AF064889

A carefully selected collection of short stories
from sixteen New Zealand writers
past and present.

Produced with the support of

ARTS COUNCIL OF NEW ZEALAND TOI AOTEAROA

LiT
Stories from Home

**EDITED BY
ELIZABETH KIRKBY-MCLEOD**

First published by OneTree House Ltd, New Zealand

© OneTree House, 2021
978-19900-350-67

All rights reserved. No part of this publication may be reproduced, stored in a retrieval system or transmitted in any form or by any means, electronic, mechanical, photocopying, recording or otherwise, without the prior permission of the publisher.

Cover design: dahlDESIGN
Printed: Your Books Wellington

8 7 6 5 4 3 2 1   1 2 3 4 5/2

CONTENTS

Foreword by Mandy Hager 7
Introduction by Elizabeth Kirkby-McLeod 11

Gina Cole .... *Baby Doll*   15
Lani Wendt Young .... *Fitu*   25
Rajorshi Chakraborti .... *Out of Zone*   31
Witi Ihimaera .... *Tent on the Home Ground*   53
Anahera Gildea .... *The Queen's chain*   65
Elsie Locke .... *The Lake and the River*   71
Owen Marshall .. *Effigies of Family Christmas*   89
David Hill .... *Free as a bird* 109
Katherine Mansfield .... *The Doll's House* 121
Patricia Grace .... *Letters from Whetu* 135
Frank Sargeson .... *A Good Boy* 157
J.P. Pomare .... *Days of Our Lives* 165
Tracey Slaughter .. *the names in the garden* 175
Russell Boey .... *Nineteen Seconds* 187
Nithya Narayanan .... *Atul* 199
Ting J. Yiu .... *Gutting* 209

Foreword
Mandy Hager

There's a very magical process that goes on when you read a story. It starts as an idea, an image, a feeling, a belief, or some other inciting spark inside a writer's head. Then the writer has to figure out who is best to tell this story (and why), where it's set, if the world is real or imaginary, and how to show that world and its characters in a real and believable way. This means looking at the society they live in, with its values, attitudes, and laws, asking who holds the power in this society or situation and why (in other words the politics of that world), and how that affects the character at the heart of the story? Then the writer downloads all these thoughts onto a page and the black marks they type or scribble build a portal into their imagination.

Now along comes you, the reader, who decodes these black marks and rebuilds the story world in your head — like a psychic exchange — and if the writer's done it well, you'll feel what the character feels, and you'll see what they see! And then the magic really kicks in, as you bring your own imagination and life experiences to the story, further enriching it and giving it a more personal meaning. It's the perfect creative collaboration!

All of these stories will excite your imagination and challenge your expectations. All these stories give you a glimpse into another life, either like yours (so you can recognise your place in it) or different (so you can put yourself in someone else's shoes.) This is the power of the story. Enter and enjoy!

Introduction
Elizabeth Kirkby-McLeod

For years I have carried around a small book simply titled *New Zealand Short Stories*. It has a blue linen hardcover and is about the size of my cellphone. Published in 1953 as part of something called "The World's Classics" it was edited by Dan Davin and printed in Oxford. It includes authors who are otherwise a mystery to me – Lady Barker and A. P. Gaskell; some more familiar, like Janet Frame and Maurice Duggan; and it has two writers you'll also find in this collection, Frank Sargeson and Katherine Mansfield (more on them soon). *New Zealand Short Stories* belonged to my father; I wouldn't be surprised if he received it from his mother. It is a treasure, a capsule of the Aotearoa New Zealand short story of the time.

My children can look forward to receiving it in their turn, for I can't throw it out or discard it. As Dan Davin says in his introduction, a short story collection throws 'a sidelight on the history of New Zealand which historical documents more narrowly conceived could hardly give.' I believe short story collections tell us something of who we think we are at the time, or imagine ourselves to be – not always the same thing.

Lit: stories from home, does not claim to be definitive, it is not an encyclopaedia of Aotearoa New Zealand short stories or even a historical review. But I hope it passes on through generations, reaching out to readers just as we reached out to bring in those two early writers, Katherine Mansfield and Frank Sargeson; just as we reached forward to find newer voices. We looked for writers who express Aotearoa New Zealand as we find ourselves now, as we imagine and think ourselves to be. First-person narratives like the stories here by Rajorshi Chakraborti and Patricia Grace allow us to glimpse Aotearoa New Zealand through the eyes of someone whose experience might not mirror our own.

One thing that I kept finding as I read was the theme of political awareness. Aotearoa New Zealanders may live far from the rest of the world, but we have never turned our backs from the injustice we see there, even as we struggle for justice at home (Mandy Hager's books *Hindsight* and *Protest!* chart those same waters in non-fiction). In the stories of Katherine Mansfield, Elsie Locke, Witi Ihimaera, Gina Cole, and Ting J. Yiu we have characters who, in unique voices, are troubled by the world as they find it; its unfairness, environmental degradation, its systems of valuing and the resulting casual degrading of life, human or otherwise. Today's students care passionately about such causes but can learn too from Tracey Slaughter's story about the impact sweeping judgment can have on individuals. Our society has much that needs to be forgiven, and much need of those who are shaped with the generosity to forgive.

Another theme I found in these stories is family. It is almost a cliché now that no person is an island, but we are all born on islands of home, siblings and caregivers, in various stages of disfunction. It is the struggles, losses and celebrations on these islands that, like for the characters in Russell Boey, Joshua Pomare and Nithya Narayanan's stories, we hold as our home-culture.

As we grow and visit different islands we begin to realise, like the characters in the stories by Anahera Gildea, David Hill, Lani Wendt Young, and Owen Marshall, that our home-culture limits, heals, defines, and forms us. At least for our beginnings. Like a good short story, the middle and ending are our own to read, our own to write.

Baby Doll
Gina Cole

I wish I have costume like Barbie. Her life so big life! We no have Barbie. We no have Barbie costume. But she have so much! She have own house, own pink car, own pink wardrobe la. Lucky I clock time card so early: 4.50 this morning. Bad story last Monday when I late on start time. They dock whole hour pay. No can lose so much money. No my fault I late. Big accident on cycle-way. Long time now, before I come many bike flow like silk ribbon in workshop when moon shine in morning. They all break bad. Nobody fix it. They take away scrap.

Now all girl walk in workshop in long line. I wait full moon make rice paddy like lamp. No moon shine last Monday. We walk on memory in dark. If you tire, if rock on path, if you new girl, la! You trip, you fall. If lucky you fall off cycle-way in soft rice paddy. Easy, you get up, carry on la. You fall on path? You hurt foot. Many girl fall and many girl hurt foot.

Last Monday one girl fall on path. I hear many scream, cry, splash. Many girl fall in rice paddy. I stop behind girl in front. I no fall in mud. We wait long time. We girl get back on path. Start moving. No girl hurt, thanks be la Allah. But … I five minute late clock time card. I say my mother, 'They dock pay this month.' I think she sad.

Today I fill quota on Black Barbie President in America. I sit straight on seat, run material in machine, sew lapel on twenty pink jacket. I see Black Barbie President in America in pink jacket in threequarter sleeve wave in crowd. I there. I, Black Queen in America, also wave in crowd in yellow jacket in three-quarter sleeve, yellow skirt. I laugh on best friend, Black Barbie President in America. One time I sew fifty jacket one run. I slow now. Pink everywhere, in air, in machine, in my hand. Material come straight in dye room. No dry, so wet. Smell in dye room catch in my throat every day. I want wash my throat kaow kaow. I want wear mask. One mask cost one week pay, no last long. Make buy, buy, buy. Pink dust catch in filter. You no breathe. Mask hot. Make pink line on mouth like you eat candy floss in market. Easy have no mask. Save one week pay, one week pay, one week pay.

My friend, she Hani girl from Yunnan Province on machine next row, orange scarf row. She big sick. Smell make girl sick we think. She go home. Girl go home ... no good. No come back. Hani girl – she die last week. We girl have sick. We girl know. Six month, cough start, you die. I start cough five month now when monsoon come, wash out cycle-way, we walk in mud. Rice worker make new cycleway. I grateful la Allah I ten year old in three week. I want die ten year old. I girl child now, nine year old.

New girl from Sichuan Province, she now on Hani girl machine. She sew tiny pink on blue flower in Hawaii lei for Black Barbie President in America make vacation, on Honolulu. She sing on Hani girl machine. Machine cry first week, bad time. Machine make strange noise, wail-on-dead noise. Girl from Sichuan make go nicely la. Sing machine first week. For sure machine run smooth. You no sing dead girl machine? For sure break down la! No make quota. You no make quota. They dock pay. You wait repair man fix it. He busy fix other girl machine. Take long time. You sit round, round. No make quota. They dock pay.

Many girl sing in room. Big room. One hundred machine. Two shift. Sichuan girl rock side, side. She sew tiny Hawaii lei, she sing Sichuan love song. I know Sichuan love song now. She teach me. I sing my machine. One song I know. Uyghur lullaby my grandmother sing long time now. I sing Uyghur lullaby every day. Lullaby help me, I make quota first week. I put magic on machine. Machine run smooth now.

My back ache. One hour we go breakfast. Kanasai I want go toilet. Must wait toilet break. I, Black Queen in America? I want go toilet break? I go la! I sew fifteen pink lapel jacket on white rim stitch. I want work on next row. Red scarf row. Girl on red scarf row sew white tank top. Next row, blue scarf row sew flare skirt. Half hour go past quick. Girl from Sichuan Province sing, she look, look on machine. Baby pile little blue on white lei on table. So pretty. Next row, green scarf row, sew Hawaii grass skirt in straw, sew Māori grass skirt in same straw. Same skirt.

Māori Barbie she make tattoo on body. When I start sew long time now, I hurt finger and blood come out. I make tattoo with blood. Funny. No hurt finger now. Now I expert. I race on Sichuan girl. I sew ten jacket, she sew ten Hawaii lei. She sew ten Hawaii lei. I cough, cough long time. She win. Not fair.

Many sewing machine in room. Big noise in room. Needle go up down, up down – big noise. I hear girl sing. Sound terrible. No sing same song. Sound horrible. Many girl rock side, side. Sore muscle. We rock side, side like river. I dizzy. I tire. Same like summer time when monsoon cloud in sky, when wind blow girl on cycle-way. Summer time we work long night, fill quota. Last summer time I sew ski jacket Black Barbie President in America make ski vacation. Ski jacket silver on pink material. I sew diamond pattern on jacket. I want work next row with Sichuan girl, orange scarf row. She sew tiny pink ski mitten, so tiny like mouse ear. She try hard, Sichuan girl big fat finger. My finger good, fast. I want make pink ski mitten, tiny doll mitten. I sit wrong row, I sit white scarf row. Next row, red scarf row, sew fluffy collar on ski jacket. Next row, black scarf row, sew pink rib waist on pink ski pant. Next row, yellow scarf row, sew glitter pink fuzz on ski pant hem. Next row, I no see it. My eye red red sore.

One morning I wake up on mat in dormitory, I find tiny pink ski mitten in night dress. I share night dress on girl from night shift. She sew in next row, orange scarf row. Same row Sichuan girl sew pink ski mitten. Must be fall down la, get stuck on girl from night shift. What I do? I take ski mitten workshop? They dock my pay! I think, think fast fast. Fold night dress ready on girl in night shift. I think President! What she do? Queen? Hawaii Princess? Oh yes la! I keep it. Secret tiny pink ski mitten from Black Barbie President in America make ski vacation. I sew pink ski mitten inside hem my shirt. Nobody see it. Nobody know. I know.

She happy make ski vacation, Black Barbie President in America. She ski down tall mountain like mountain in Yunnan Province. Sichuan girl tell me she see mountain in Yunnan Province. I, Black Queen in America in fluffy yellow collar on silver jacket, in yellow ski pant. I ski down mountain loop, loop, loop. Huge snow fall on feet. Crazy snow, giant pattern. Snow pattern on plastic box on packing line. We ski, Black Barbie President in America, Princess Hawaii Barbie, Doctor Barbie. Doctor Barbie she fix my cough. We fall down mountain laugh, laugh, laugh.

Many girl my shift, we go breakfast break. We stand long line one cup rice, dry fish. I hungry oh. I think I want eat fried rice and Coke. I sit under mango tree. Many girl sit under mango tree. Girl from Sichuan Province rock side, side, eat, eat. We talk. Want make quota. Go home family. We eat slow make food go long way. Ten minute, end breakfast break. I see green mango hang on my head. I touch mango like belly, smooth, cool. My breath come slow, noisy like dragon roar in out, in out. I no here on mango gold, ready for eat. I no here.

Breakfast finish. I lean on machine, put head down on rest. I dream spring time. Rice high. Rice noisy in wind. My row, white scarf row, sew blue silk epaulette, Air Force One jacket. Tiny, tiny material we sew on gold. Many girl keep time like river. My row sew eight blue epaulette, red scarf row sew eight brass button, blue scarf row eight zipper, green row eight box pleat, purple row eight waist band, orange scarf row eight cuff. On, on, one girl faint. They dock girl pay. We stop few minute. Other girl go her seat. We start. One girl make sleep, sew finger. Blood fall on Barbie jacket. They dock girl pay. I like Air Force One jacket.

I, Black Queen in America jump out Air Force One. I wear yellow silk jacket, pink epaulette, pink helmet like Pop Up Parachute Barbie, free. No one stop me.

'Hey! Wake up Baby Doll!'

Girl from Sichuan Province shout at me. I wake up. Malaysian boss lady she high up la. Far away. She look like Malaysian Barbie. Perfect face. She no see me sleep, far away, no binocular, like Opera Barbie.

My row change. Now sew pink inauguration gown. I ask girl from Sichuan province what this mean 'inauguration'.

She say, 'You no work, no sew button on jacket, you take toilet break anytime. You Princess.'

This gown ... big work. I think Black Barbie President in America no like it. Inauguration gown so heavy so hot. Many frill. Neck so high, train so long like Princess Barbie wedding gown. I sew ten long train. I race Sichuan girl. She sew ten long white glove. I squeeze tiny pink ski mitten hide in hem. I see big life, many friend. We laugh. Best, best friend Black Barbie President in America make me Princess. Doctor Barbie she fix my cough. Pop Up Parachute Barbie she make me fly.

I dream my inauguration.

'Baby Doll' was first published in Gina Cole's short story collection, **Black Ice Matter** (Huia, 2016).

Writer Gina Cole is of Fijian, Scottish and Welsh descent. She won the Best First Book Award at the 2017 Ockham NZ Book Awards for her story collection *Black Ice Matter*. Her work has been widely anthologized and has appeared in numerous publications including takahē, JAAM, Express Magazine, Span, Landfall, Geometry, The Three Lamps, and Ora Nui. She is a qualified lawyer and practised law for many years. She has an LLB(Hons) and an MJur from the University of Auckland. She is an Honorary Fellow in Writing at the University of Iowa. She has a Master of Creative Writing degree from the University of Auckland and a PhD in Creative Writing from Massey University.

Fitu

Lani Wendt Young

I am going to my first teenage party. There will be music, dancing, food and boys. A birthday for a girl in my class at school. I don't know her very well. She has parties often and this is the first time I've been invited. Probably because it's my first time scoring high enough in exams to come first in class. If you can't be pretty, rich or good at sports, then you can still get invited to parties if you are clever.

I'm wearing black high heels, a denim skirt and a top with sparkles on it. I'm nervous about the heels. What if I trip?

My father sits me down for a serious talk before he drives me to the party. A talk about not behaving like 'those afakasi'. The rich ones. The afakasi who have parties and invite each other to them. Who dress a certain way. Talk a certain way. Act a certain way. According to my father, our family doesn't belong to that afakasi crowd because his father was a bus driver who grew taro on the side.

"They've always looked down on us and our branch of the aiga," says my father.

"We're not like them," warns my father. "We may have a palagi last name but we have never been accepted by them. We don't do the things they do. Or talk the way they do. Be careful and remember, you're not like them."

I am afakasi but not like those other afakasi. Right, got it, Dad.

Because being afakasi is about more than having a palagi last name. Yes, it means you have a palagi ancestor somewhere back on the tree. (Not a Chinese one or a meauli one.) But there are many kinds of afakasi.

There are rich afakasi families and poor ones. There are light-skinned afakasi and dark ones. There are the afakasi who are infamous for having many children from many different women. My mother has a theory. "They're stuck with the colonial-days attitude where white men thought they could have sex with whoever they wanted to. Whenever they wanted to." She tells us, "Never marry a man from that family. He would never be faithful to you."

There are afakasi families who are famous for being eye-catchingly gorgeous. The men are movie-star handsome.

The women are beautiful with fair skin, light hair, and palagi eyes and noses. They win pageants, become flight attendants, have their pick of the men in Apia.

There are afakasi families with buildings and plantations named after them. Whose forebears did deals that gave them vast land holdings. There are afakasi who have #nextToHeaven status because they donated land to their church, they have sons who are faifeau and priests, they have daughters who are serving God as nuns in faraway lands.

And then there are afakasi like us.

"What kind of afakasi are we?" I ask my father. But I already know the answer. Because I've heard it all my life.

"The Samoan kind of afakasi." Then he adds, with our family's usual brand of intellectual uppity-ness, "And the academic kind. We may be poor but we're smart. We get scholarships and university degrees. Everybody knows this." I think about my first-place-in-class achievement, the family's satisfaction at seeing the photo in the newspaper of me accepting my trophies at prize-giving, and I nod in agreement. In that moment we are united in that most Samoan of traits. Fia-show. Appearances and family reputation are everything.

My mother chooses that moment to make a snort of derision. "There's not much point being clever if you can't use it to make money though, is there? *We're poor but we're smart.* So useless."

She's obviously having a bad day. One of her, *It's such a hard life in this country ... being married to this man and his family ... looking after his children ...*

My father and I exchange a look. Commiseration. She just doesn't understand. Because she's not Samoan.

'Fitu' was first published in Lani Wendt Young's collection **Afakasi Woman** (OneTree House, 2019).

Lani Wendt Young is a Samoan/Maori author of the popular Telesā series, and is also a columnist. She's worked as a scriptwriter for Disney and her stories for children are published by the NZ School Journal.

She was the 2018 recipient of the Douglas Gabb Australia-Pacific Journalism internship and in 2017 her reporting on climate change issues in the Pacific won her a coveted fellowship award covering the UN Climate Conference in Bonn, Germany. Lani gave to annual NZ Book Council Lecture in 2019, and in 2018 she was named the ACP Pacific Laureate.

Out of Zone

Rajorshi Chakraborti

This had been Sajida's morning mission – to drive up to Karori after dropping off the girls, for a 10 o' clock meeting with three women she didn't know, in order to ask if they were interested in renting out or selling their late mother's house to a Bangladeshi stranger who'd showed up at their door.

It had in fact been even more absurd and hopeless than that. See if you can keep up. Prompted probably by Abir's recounting of yet another futile bid they had submitted - their 33rd overall - for a house in Wilton that went for $275,000 above its registered value, Raj, a regular customer at the Victoria Street branch of their restaurant (whom Sajida had never met, because she looked after Newtown), had mentioned to Abir that a place might be coming up for sale on his street in Karori. An elderly neighbour of his had passed away sometime before, and her three daughters, who each lived in a different city overseas (London, Hong Kong and somewhere else), had finally been able to gather in Wellington, first to organise a memorial service for their mother and then to make a decision about her house. Abir had jumped at this half-glimpse of a possibility, at the thought of having a head-start on the competition before any ads appeared, and perhaps especially at the image of the sisters grabbing the chance for a quick sale, eager as they would be to return to their lives and families. Who wouldn't want to avoid the hassle of a drawn-out sale process, especially if you were three siblings settled overseas and the person who'd showed up was making an incredibly fair offer, very much in line with what places were going for in the area, but without the extra weeks of waiting, the steep estate agent fees, or the prospect of possible return trips to New Zealand?

Of course, this was all Abir talking, as he immediately, and passionately, urged Raj to arrange a meeting with the sisters, while formulating on the spot the very arguments he hoped to present to them.

'And you must also mention that we are a good Bangladeshi family, of South Asian origin just as they are, running two renowned restaurants in Wellington and with beautiful daughters aged ten and twelve. And that our top priority at this moment, and we're being entirely frank with you, is to enter the zone for Wellington City High where Runa would be eligible to go from next February. Which is to say – and this is the point to emphasise, Raj – that if a sale seems too big a decision to agree upon after such a recent demise of their beloved mother and with all of them so far away, and so many memories associated with the house in which they too must have grown up, then the sisters need to know that we would also be happy to rent. No pressure at all, you make sure to say; in fact, renting the house to us could buy them precious time in which to plan their next step.'

'They didn't grow up in that house. Their mother moved there four years ago, after the death of her husband. Although it still has three bedrooms so that the daughters could visit with their kids.'

'In that case, our role is to be the temporary custodians of their mother's memory. You need to exaggerate nothing, Raj. When you call them, you only describe what you see of us and the girls after school every time you visit the restaurant, how they study here and help out in the kitchen. These are the people who will be looking after their mother's home, another family hoping to build a life with our daughters exactly as their parents did a generation ago.'

Sajida of course hadn't witnessed any of these exchanges

between Abir and their unknown well-wisher, but they had been described and re-enacted for her with painstaking detail at home and in the car. And each of the three times Raj had visited the Victoria Street restaurant during this delicate period – they had just ten days before two of the three sisters departed, leaving one in charge of executing any decisions – his meals had, it went without saying, been on the house.

But then last night, fifteen hours before the all-important meeting which Raj had finally been able to secure, Abir had called Sajida – from his branch to hers, at a time when both of them had customers and were therefore unable to discuss, let alone argue, anything ¬– with the apparently sudden brainwave that she should go alone the next morning, so that the first meeting could be a 'woman-to-women, mother-to-mothers thing' (as he put it in Bengali). Here was his chain of 'logic': 'Two of the sisters are mothers, you're obviously all daughters, and we're doing this for our daughters. They have just lost their mother. It is genuinely an all-women situation, and they'll be able to see how much this means to you. Afterwards, of course I'll come. For the second meeting we'll even take Runa and Pori along, so that they can see who all this haste is for.'

'Raj and you came up with this plan together. How is it an all-women situation?'

'Uff, it will be all-women tomorrow when you're there.

Don't you see the impact of that? It will show them what kind of family we are, why our daughters' education is so important to us. Raj told me two of the sisters, including the one who is staying behind, have PhDs. The third is in pharmaceuticals marketing.'

Abir had time to mention that in the middle of an evening shift, but not thereafter to listen to Sajida's counter-arguments about why they needed to go together. Apparently the new Czech girl had got another order wrong, and had served a chicken tikka starter to a customer who was expecting the tikka masala with its gravy to go with his naan.

***

She'd knocked, been invited in and offered a seat at the dining table where all three sisters gathered around her, while behind them, throughout her stay, a man with an iPad photographed and documented furniture that was apparently all going to an auction house. There were some exquisite things, including the dining set itself, which was made of finely carved wood, probably from Rajasthan. Sajida's first thought had been – how fine all this would look at the restaurant.

Don't move them until you've heard me out, she wanted to say, but reminded herself: we were expecting the house to be unfurnished. It's probably better for our offer this way. And Sajida, you can't ask about the furniture as well this morning, no matter how beautiful, not when you've come to talk about the house. You'll seem ruthless and grasping.

Although as she was sitting down it had hit her more strongly than ever before that she was about to mention a huge sum of money in relation to a house she had just stepped into for the first time, and which she'd recognised from the outside solely because Runa had shown it to them using Street View. What were they doing? They would NEVER buy a restaurant space this way.

Well, say that after you've bid for 33 restaurant spaces, Sajida.

In fairness to them, the women heard her out. Raj for his three free meals had mostly primed them accurately. By the by, it turned out that the furniture was from Malaysia, which was also where the girls' parents had migrated from, as opposed to South Asia as Abir had assumed in his stirring demo speech, just from learning the late owner's name. Well, only slightly South Asia, because the oldest did say 'Mum and Dad's families had been Jaffna Tamils, like a century ago.'

But the sisters were all born and raised here, in Wellington, just up the road in a bigger house, although Sajida didn't need to be told this. Everything from their accents to 'Mum and Dad' made this clear. I really wish you were here, Abir, to see this 'South Asian all-women's connection'.

She made sure to mention the top-priority zoning issue

regarding Wellington City High as well as the option of renting. I'm totally following the script, Abir, Sajida thought, as she pulled out a restaurant card with their phone numbers. I even said the number 33, just as you instructed.

'Please let us know if you come to any decision, or, if you want to talk more, do come for a meal to either restaurant, any time except Sunday afternoon.'

From the moment I saw them, I had expected them to be snobs, Sajida acknowledged to herself afterwards in the car. And if she put herself in their shoes, some stranger from across town eager to get their foot in the door before anyone else having heard about her mother's death – how would she have reacted?

In fact, not once had Abir suggested that she begin by asking whether they were even thinking of selling the place, and it hadn't occurred to her either.

But the sisters had seemed friendly enough while she spoke, and afterwards they said that Raj's multiple phone calls had actually helped them reach a decision, for which they were indirectly grateful to Abir and Sajida. They had realised that at least for the immediate future they were neither ready to sell nor rent out the place, and had instead reached a compromise arrangement. They were going to look for a tenant who needed the house only for the next ten months, because they would like to return to Wellington with their families in January, gather here for a few weeks next summer from London, Hong Kong and Vancouver (that was the third place).

And before Sajida could respond to this, the Hong Kong one who was the middle sister added that luckily, just this morning, their next-door neighbour had rung to say one of his best friends needed somewhere to stay for the rest of the year before heading off to travel in South America around Christmas. Which would be perfect timing.

'It wouldn't really have worked for a family, would it, to have to vacate your home within ten months, and not to know what our longer-term plans will be,' London offered by way of consolation. She was the oldest. Vancouver had disappeared a few minutes ago, apparently to help the furniture-lister.

'Which means we need to thank you, because your approach helped us reach a decision, otherwise you can imagine – an endless round of conference calls on Skype, and when are we ever all awake and available at the same time?' This was London again; of her friendliness there could be no doubt.

Hong Kong wanted to know 'But what's so special about Wellington City High? Where are the girls zoned to go just now?'

'Actually South Wellington High School is fine, but Kiwi

parents who have grown up here have mentioned to us several times – try to get into Wellington City if your priority is academics. They are the ones who suggested renting something temporarily if we have to.'

Hong Kong saw fit to mention at this point that all three of them had attended the private girls' school in Karori. London more sensitively stepped in to say that these were big problems in England as well, with parents resorting to some desperate measures to be in line for their preferred schools, but that in her opinion, if Sajida and Abir liked their present house, they should stay where they were, because 'in any case, the most important thing is the home environment, isn't it? That's where learning is truly reinforced.'

Sajida nodded, and had a fleeting picture of Runa and Pori's evenings at one of the tables in the Victoria Street restaurant. They certainly did some studying there, with Abir supervising in between looking after customers, but it probably wasn't London's image of an ideal home environment.

It was as Sajida was getting up that she noticed for the first time what must have been their mother's portrait, on a coffee table right beside where she had slipped off her shoes. Would mentioning that earlier have made a difference?

Slightly in a trance she spoke her first lines at this meeting that had not been scripted.

'My mother is entirely bedridden in Bangladesh. She has

Alzheimer's and failing kidneys. I need to go to her, but we have this second restaurant now to raise funds for the new house, and for my mother's care and treatment. I'm very sorry for your loss.'

Hong Kong and London commiserated (they did have names – coincidentally all beginning with S – which Sajida had failed to latch on to and had been counting on asking Raj if the meeting went anywhere). Vancouver, who'd turned up at the door, said Mum too had suffered in her last few months. Near the end she hardly ate.

They stood at the doorstep as Sajida walked to her car. Even though she had doubts about it, before she got in she asked when the furniture auction would be.

'Oh, this ghastly stuff?' London had laughed. 'We just want it out of the house. This was all Mum and Dad. If you came back next week you'd see how large and light the rooms really are. These brothel-like curtains are going too.'

'Within the next two weeks,' Vancouver answered her question. 'I have your number. I can message you the details.'

Sajida thanked them and got into the car. If she mentioned this furniture sale, Abir would almost certainly use it as a pretext to call once more. She should let him have that chance, even if she still couldn't describe the house beyond the living room.

***

It was the corner grove that made her stop; she'd seen nothing else at first beyond the initial rise of the street. She had been daydreaming while driving that one day Runa and Pori would be settled in London and Vancouver, in which case would she and Abir choose to remain in Wellington, or return at least for part of each year to Pabna? The car clock said 10.31; she didn't need to be at the restaurant for another hour. Gulabji, the Newtown chef, knew she might be late this morning. This had been arranged in the hope of a successful discussion, but she'd come out in under twenty minutes, and was now on her way to Victoria Street to file her report with Abir.

On the left-hand corner of that last side road were three coconut palms! Not the usual native tree ferns with their deceptively similar trunks; no, those fronds and the hanging fruit were unmistakable. But also, around them and leading up the side road, Sajida had noticed several other trees and bushes that looked equally out of place here and yet were extremely familiar to her – jaba (hibiscus), krishnachura (no idea what that was called in English), bougainvillea.

She had hurriedly indicated and pulled over into a space twenty metres down Glenmore St, because, to put it simply even if it sounded strange, somebody's garden in the middle of Wellington had suddenly transported her to Bangladesh!

Someone, probably from South Asia, or else Indonesia or Malaysia, or perhaps somewhere like Fiji or Samoa, which were also quite warm as far as Sajida knew, had succeeded in creating in this unlikely climate a little spot straight from their homeland.

It was while checking the road before getting out that another possibility came to her. The Botanic Gardens were directly across the street: this might well be their initiative, to plant in the vicinity some of the countless seeds they held from around the world. Or, might some seeds have blown over and somehow flourished just in this corner?

Whatever the reason, Sajida thought as she pulled out her phone to take a picture, she wanted to have a moment to savour this magical feeling. They hardly ever passed through this part of town, but probably other passersby who were also from hot countries were routinely reminded of home going past this particular grove. And if it was a small extension of the Botanics, then they needed to visit the main gardens as soon as possible, the next free Sunday when there wasn't an open home to attend. Because Abir too would love this sense of closing, then reopening his eyes and not quite believing what was still there! There might be a whole area across the street devoted to tropical plants. How come none of their friends or customers had mentioned it before?

But what happened next was so astonishing that at first

Sajida forgot to record anything on her phone. Without thinking about it, she had walked a few metres up the footpath along the side road, which, after an initial steep portion, flattened and broadened considerably, and now from its crest, she discovered that the road led to what looked like a dark green pond up ahead, that was fringed by coconut palms all the way around and a few banana trees as well, exactly as a pond would be in a village back home.

How was this possible? This time Sajida turned around to be reassured that New Zealand was still within walking distance, the busy main road she expected to see thirty metres behind her in chilly, windy Wellington situated far from the tropics - Glenmore Street, on which if she had gone in the other direction, she would have arrived at the former Chinese embassy and the main entrance to the Botanics. How could such a landscape be here? How could a single spot in the shade of a big hill receive enough heat to become Bangladesh?

Yes, Bangladesh, and not Indonesia or Fiji, she now felt confident of saying, because two further surprises had only just become apparent, in rapid succession, that exceeded even the pond and all the vegetation.

Up here, along the flat, wide portion of this impossible cul-de-sac that began in a Wellington Sajida could still turn around and confirm – a green Metlink bus went past right then, and there was the fence of the Botanics – but somehow ended in rural Sirajganj or Pabna, the houses too weren't the usual Thorndon cottages of Glenmore Street or the other side roads up ahead. (They had attended two open homes in the area, for a flat and a cottage, both turning out to be three-bedroom only in name, but they'd been within walking distance of Wellington City High). No, what Sajida was taking in with disbelief on either side of her were huts of mud and thatch, partially hidden behind all the lovely, thick foliage, but so much like home that even most of home wasn't like this anymore. This was the Bangladesh of Sajida's childhood, of folktales, children's books and songs, a village of exactly the sort she often wished Runa and Pori could stay in during their short, rushed, usually bi-annual trips home. And, as if to confirm her sense of stepping into the past she noticed just then that the road she was standing on was no longer paved, and hadn't been beyond the opening few metres down at the turn-off, and also that further ahead on the right-hand edge of the pond was a woman in an everyday sari doing her washing, as though this was simply what one did at 10.40 on a Wednesday morning in central Wellington.

The woman, possibly Sajida's age or younger, was squatting facing the pond, and at first Sajida wanted to flee. She even took a few backward steps, but then stopped, looked around to see if anyone was watching her from inside one of the huts, and once more took out her phone. Her first thought was to call Abir, but she decided against speaking loudly just then. That could wait; she'd call him from the car. Right now, the priority was to record, before it all disappeared, before the morning became normal again. As she moved the camera downwards from the houses and trees before her, she realised that even the soil here was dusty and dry, as it would be in March at home! Hé Allah.

And yet, I'm not feeling any warmer, was Sajida's very next thought, as she completed a slow full circle of filming to take in everything around. Which means this must still be Wellington, otherwise the sun would already be unbearable.

Vancouver, London and Hong Kong had had recycling today, she also recalled as she filmed. Their black and yellow bin had been on the pavement along with a rubbish bag. She switched off the camera and looked around to follow up this odd thought. No, not a single wheelie bin on this Wellington street, nor were there any cars. She could still hear vehicles going up and down Glenmore Street, she thought, sounding like a far-off sea; and there her own car key was, in her handbag, where she had put it less than five minutes ago. But not a single home-owner (or rather, hut-owner) on this street seemed to possess a car, which was exactly as it would have been in the rural Pabna of her mother's childhood.

Playing back the footage she had just recorded had a calming, strengthening effect on Sajida, its mere existence on her phone, a forty-five second clip that confirmed through replication this unbelievable scene she had wandered into. Of course she would speak to that woman. It was the most natural thing to do, and the only way for her questions to be answered. How straightforward this option suddenly seemed, and how absurd her thought of running away a couple of minutes before. Fifteen steps, and one question in Bengali, and everything would become clear.

The woman didn't turn around even when Sajida was directly behind her.

'Achcha, can I go to Karori this way,' she asked, although what Sajida had wanted to confirm was what country they were in. But at the last moment it seemed too weird a question to spring on someone, as though it was Sajida who had just landed from outer space. In any case, wouldn't this much more normal query, posed in Bengali, clarify everything she sought to know?

'You can, but it's a roundabout way with ups and downs. And there are many steps,' the woman replied in Bengali as fluent as Sajida's. She was holding a man's shirt from which she had been wringing out the water.

Sajida was trying to hide her astonishment, process the meaning of this response, and decide what to say next all at once, because her speaking Bengali and yet knowing the way to Karori meant not one thing, but two.

They were in Bangladesh and in Wellington at the same time!

Unless a group of Bangladeshis had managed to recreate village life from back home in this corner of Thorndon, and chose to live this way. But that was impossible, and she and Abir would surely have heard about it.

The woman too had been sizing Sajida up, although she didn't look unfriendly. She was younger as well, which gave Sajida some confidence.

'Where are you coming from?'

'Just back there,' was all Sajida could vaguely say.

'Who are you looking for?'

'No ... no one. I was merely going past. I, we ... are in fact looking for a house, to be near my daughters' school.' Before the woman had a chance to reply, Sajida added 'Do you know if there are any homes available here?'

The woman thought for a while, then said there was nothing she could think of 'in this neighbourhood', but where was Sajida actually from?

'Uh, Pabna, Munshiganj, Wellington. I have lived in all these places. But now Rongotai, near the airport. Do you know Wellington well?'

'A little. I don't go out that often. But the best way to go to Karori is definitely up that main road. Do you want me to show you?'

'No, thank you. I know that way. I wondered if there was a short cut. But tell me, if I come back here tomorrow, will you still be here?'

'If it's not raining, probably. I can ask my husband this afternoon if he knows of any vacant houses.'

The woman got up off her haunches, gave the shirt she was holding a couple more squeezes, then threw it into a tin pail Sajida hadn't noticed. Now she sat herself down on a flat rock so that she could face Sajida, who stood a few feet away.

'But I don't think you'll like it here,' she added, smiling. Sajida felt sure she was referring to her jacket, jeans, and shoes.

For the third time, or maybe more, since they had begun speaking, the same strange thing happened inside Sajida. Everything she'd wanted to ask was intended to be subtle and indirect, yet each question that came out of her mouth was almost unimaginably blunt. Harsh, abrupt, terribly phrased. Anyone might take offence at such provocations. What if the woman yelled out in anger to her neighbours?

'Achcha, have I died? Is this paradise?'

Thankfully, that made her laugh.

'That you like the place is good to know, but no, you haven't died.'

'Are you my mother?' Again! This was worse than rash. The woman would shortly call for help, to protect herself from a mad person!

But she had evidently decided to humour Sajida as the safest way to see her off.

'Do I resemble her?'

Then Sajida was proved wrong once more, because the woman asked her if she would like to sit down for a while inside her house. And it was Sajida who refused, who was afraid and said 'No, I better leave,' who turned half her body towards Glenmore Street as she spoke.

'Then come back another day. Bring your daughters with you.'

'There are no free days besides Sundays, and Sundays go by endlessly searching for a house.'

Sajida's excuse was genuine, something she might say almost out of reflex to any new acquaintance. The woman raised her hand to say goodbye.

'I will come one Sunday. Abir can go by himself to a few viewings. But, will you really still be here?'

'Where will we go? That's my house, if I'm not here,' and she pointed to Sajida's left, to a hut behind a banana grove.

'I will definitely come. But I'd better go now, as the restaurant will open shortly.' Finally Sajida was saying things that she recognised, that were normal, that she might have said to a friend on the phone, and as she spoke, she realised that she no longer felt afraid. 'This was wonderful. I was going past, and I stopped to take a look, and it's been incredible.'

'Bring your daughters soon,' the woman replied. 'The lychee season is coming. They can have as many as they like.'

'Certainly. Then there will be mangoes,' Sajida said, also with a laugh, again without expecting to, but this time with no embarrassment.

'And I'll bring along some food as well. You must try my cooking,' she added just before waving and turning around.

Sajida had already taken a few steps when she remembered the supply of restaurant cards she was carrying for the morning's meeting. She walked back to the woman, who had begun to wring a vest, and placed the card on the rock she had been sitting on.

'You can also visit me whenever you like,' Sajida said. 'I am always at the Newtown branch.'

An earlier version of 'Out of Zone' was published on the website **Juggernaut** (2017).

Rajorshi Chakraborti is an Indian-born novelist, essayist and short-story writer. He is the author of six novels and a collection of short fiction, including, most recently, the novel *Shakti* that appeared in 2020. He lives in Wellington with his family.

Tent on the Home Ground

Witi Ihimaera

George had been drinking in the pub with his friends for about twenty minutes when, from out of the smoke, Api pounced on him like a panther.

"Aren't I good enough for your mates?" Api said.

George was taken aback. He hadn't seen Api since they'd quarrelled at Te Huinga. "I don't know what you mean," he answered. "It's good to see you, Api. Been a long time."

Api laughed. Mocking. Scornful. "Well I've been sitting over there ever since you came in," he said. "Watching you. You and your mates." He jerked his head at the others at the table.

"I didn't see you," George answered.

"You didn't want to," Api said.

"So why didn't you come over to me?" George flared. "Bit of a snob aren't you?"

"I know when I'm not wanted," Api answered.

George gave a gesture of helplessness. Api would never change. What was the use. All this suspicion. All this distrust. The wonder was that they were still friends.

He introduced Api to the others: Peter, Warren and David, all from the office where he worked. All members of the establishment that Api so despised. White collar. Middle class. The people climbing to the top. Elitist.

"I've seen you around," David said. He put out his hand and Api gripped it in a test of strength. David gave a nervous smile.

Api filled his glass from a jug on the table. "Up the lot of you," he saluted.

"Quit it, Api," George said.

"And up you too, mate," Peter interrupted. He had met Api before and their antipathy for each other was obvious. Polarised from the beginning by their different backgrounds neither would give an inch to the other. Their meetings had always been characterised by the clash of flint against flint.

Hastily, George separated them. "Look here you two,"

he said. "I came in here to have a nice quiet drink. Now simmer down." He started to make small talk with Warren. The atmosphere began to cool, relax and spread itself out comfortably as if a belt had been let out a couple of notches. George smiled at Api. While Warren was talking with Peter and David, he turned to Api and said:

"You know, it really is good to see you, Api."

Api shrugged his shoulders. "What's the celebration? It's not like you to come to the pub, brother."

"David's been promoted," George answered. "He's leaving us at the end of the week."

"And you?" Api asked. "You been promoted too?" There was a hint of derision in the words. Behind dark glasses Api's eyes pricked George with ill-concealed mockery.

"No," George answered.

"So you haven't been sucked into the system," Api said. "Not all the way yet."

"They don't want me," George returned.

Apparently he still didn't fit in, still appeared to lack that special sense of administrative ability and those nebulous qualities which interviewers were instructed to seek out in those applying for promotion. What the hell. He was happy enough where he was anyway.

"George should have been promoted though," David said to Api with a quick, anxious smile.

At his words, Api exploded with anger. "Don't you patronise us, man."

"Api..." George began.

But once Api was started he was difficult to stop. His temper flashed out like a paw.

"Of course my brother should have been promoted," he said. "But he's a black man and this is a white system. And does the white man want us in positions of power? Like hell he does."

"Hey, easy there," Warren interrupted.

"Look," David began. "I didn't mean to..."

"No, you look," Api growled, "You take a good hard look at the system you've created. It's in your image, not ours. Everything about it is white. Religion. Education. Politics. You name it. And I'll bet you there's hardly any of us in it. Why? Because you're scared of us. So you keep us down. At the bottom of the system. Eh. Eh." The words cracked like breaking bones.

"Crap," Peter muttered.

"What did you say?" Api asked dangerously.

"Forget it, Api," George said. "Peter, just shut up won't you? Both of you, drink up."

But Peter took no notice. "I said crap and I mean crap," he said again. "Just because you can't cope with the system, Api, you accuse it of being racist."

"Hell, that's because it is," Api answered.

"Prove it then," Peter said.

Api began to laugh. His laughter rose above the hum of conversations in the pub, catching the attention of a few people in the crowded bar. Momentarily diverted, they watched Api curiously before returning to their drinking.

"What's the joke?" Peter said angrily.

"You," Api answered. "You ask for proof and there's so much of it I don't know where to begin."

Because there isn't any," Peter said.

Api narrowed his eyes. Then he flashed the quick smile of a panther. "Who discovered New Zealand?" he asked.

"Eh? Oh, Abel Tasman," Peter answered startled.

Api grinned with triumph. "Man," he said. "Your answer is your proof. Long before Abel Tasman got here, Kupe discovered this country. But you've probably never heard of him, have you. After all, he was only a Maori."

Peter reddened with anger. "Kupe? He's just a legend."

"Your second proof," Api answered. "Anything that happened to us you call myth or legend. Anything that happened to you is called history. Cheers man. You better shut your mouth by drinking up."

By now, Api was in a tremendous humour. He drained his glass and winked at George. Then he turned to Peter and said:

"How about buying us another round, friend?"

Peter looked at him with eyes gleaming. "Buy your own," he said.

For a moment, George thought that Api would lash out with his fists. But no, Api was enjoying the extent of Peter's antipathy.

"Don't be like that," Api mocked. "Buy your brother another drink."

Api. Circling Peter with his calculated comments. Teasing. Trying to draw Peter further out into the open. Waiting.

"Lay off him," George warned Api.

But it was too late. Peter had had enough. "You see racism in everything, don't you?" he said to Api. "The system as you call it. Everything. And only because you haven't been able to make it."

"The system won't let me," Api taunted.

"Why not? Everybody goes through it. All of us must face it. But you? Oh no. You want to pull it down. Well you'll never do it."

Api's eyelids flickered with growing anger.

"Yes," Peter continued scornfully. "I've seen you and your friends down at Parliament. You've set up an embassy down there haven't you? To protest for Maori rights, isn't it? Well, there's some of us who think you already have more rights than we have. And we all think your protest is a big laugh. A joke."

"Come off it, Peter," George said uneasily. "Api, don't listen to him. It's the beer talking."

But Api was moving in for the kill. "You think you're so superior," he said to Peter. "Well, laugh while you can, man. The world won't be yours much longer. Maori rights? Man, we're protesting for human rights. And we want the white system to acknowledge our rights. We're no joke, man. And we're hitting you at the heart of your system. Parliament itself. Your home ground, man. And we'll win too. You've raped us long enough."

"For God's sake, Api," George said. "Enough of that talk."

Api turned on him. "As for you, brother, whose side are you going to be on?"

"It's not a question of taking sides," George answered. "It's not a matter of winning or losing."

"So," Api mocked. "Still sitting on that bloody fence. Come off it, brother. With me. Now."

"You do things your way, Api," George said. "I'll do things my way."

"How?" Api asked. "You'll never get the chance. You'll never be promoted. We can't make it from the inside so we have to hit the system from the outside. Can't you see that?"

George closed his eyes. When he opened them he saw Api

putting down his glass. Api's face was filled with contempt.

"Up the lot of you," he said. Then he walked away. Silent. Padding out of the pub.

For a long time nobody spoke at the table. Then David and Warren began to relax. It was all over now.

"Well," George sighed. He grinned at Peter.

"The black bastard," Peter swore.

"Hey . . ." George began.

"The black bastard," Peter swore again. "He'll never win."

The words punched into George's mind. It wasn't a question of winning or losing. It wasn't a matter of white against black. It wasn't a question of taking sides. Or was it? And if it was, which side was the winner and which side was the loser?

"Shut up, Peter," George growled. "Shut up. And buy us another round, brother. Forget what's happened. For God's sake."

Outside, the night grew dark. Don at Parliament, a tent had been pitched on the home ground. A banner flapped on a wooden fence: You Stole My Land Now Leave My Soul. From within the tent came the sound of a guitar, singing and laughter. The sounds did not seem aggressive at all. We're protesting for human rights.

George stood watching from the shadows. He had been there over twenty minutes. Then he walked to the tent, past a placard bearing an upraised hand, and opened the flap.

The light from a tilley lamp blazed upon him. He'll never win, the black bastard, Peter had sworn. The guitar stopped. The people in the tent looked at him. Curious. Wary. In the corner was Api. George tried to smile.

"Api, aren't I good enough for your mates," he said.

'Tent on the Home Ground' was first published in Witi Ihimaera's collection **The New Net Goes Fishing** (Heinemann, 1977).

Witi Ihimaera is of Māori descent and is regarded as one of New Zealand's leading writers. He was the first Māori writer to have a book of short stories and a novel published in the 1970s, and 'Tent on the Home Ground' is one of his earliest published stories. Since then he has written a number of important and award winning books including *The Whale Rider*, *Bulibasha King of the Gypsies* and *Māori Boy*. His latest book is *Navigating the Stars*. He lives in Auckland.

The Queen's chain

Anahera Gildea

My mother was born in the summer of '53, as the Queen took her first steps on our soil. Nan cursed and swore cos she never got to see nothin' – not even from the hospital where the patients crowded at the windows to watch the landaulette pass by. But she named her daughter Elizabeth anyway; they all did.

That's how the women do it in our line – I got my name, Te Ao Haere, cos I was born straight into the '75 land march, well, close as intention can get you. My mother liked to think she supported her people with each push and each bear-down that forced me out.

As soon as she was allowed, she squashed the whole world down into a single vinyl suitcase and slid us both into the car like she was trying to get us back in the womb.

'Back to the land!' she shouted. 'Back to our roots!' And she left, swearing at the city behind us.

Our house was built in the '50s by my grandfather before the rest of the street got built up round it. The land came through from Nan, from the Raukawa whānau. It started where my feet hit the kerb and finished up at the creek down the back. On the day my mother and I arrived to move in, the lawn was newly mowed and there were rough broom marks on the path from the wire gate to the doorsteps. Blades of grass blew onto and off the concrete as we walked towards Nan at the door. Overgrown shrubs and foreign grasses ate away at the foot of every wall and crawled up the back fence.

When I was old enough to keep my gumboots on, it got to be my job to help her drag the weeds to the pile down the back. She would talk to me about each of the flowers as we passed like they were her other children. There was red roses and hot-pink dahlias, jonquils and tulips, lilies and irises, and falling-over ranunculuses. She reckoned the smell of a flower in the last minutes of its life was the best, most amazing thing.

'When you were born, you were sick.' When my mother gardened, all the pretty stuff would let her thinking out.

The Queen's chain

'We stayed in the hospital, just you and me, and you had to get fed from a tube.'

She never looked at me when she was telling, she just went back into herself and remembered out loud.

'I would line up beside the other women in a little room on a chair facing the wall. We had these new electric pumps with long rubber tentacles on them that you pulled out and attached to your breasts.' She would show this bit by waving her arms around and I would laugh, kind of faking it.

'Everyone would just stare at the wall, and no one would talk directly with each other cos women were more modest then.'

Whenever she paused to clear the space around a plant, I would just wait and then she'd go on again like she'd never stopped.

'The sound of the milk hitting the plastic catch bottle and the chug of the machine was like strange music in that quiet room. Suck chug spray. Suck chug spray. I would collect as many bottles as I could fill, and we would all keep looking at that wall while we put the lids on, taking off the tentacles and mopping up our spills.'

Then the bad moment would come, and she would get sad and confess, 'I didn't breastfeed you.'

'I know, it's all good, Mum. No one cares,' I would whisper but she never heard me. You can't hear the dead, I reckon.

'But I did my best,' she would finish.

Eventually the view from the road became of lilies curving up around the path and shooting heavenward, like it was them that held up the walls, the stamens yearning forward, inviting the touch that got coloured fingermarks pasted across clothes.

'Never a dull moment round here, Te Ao,' my mother would say, with the air of someone who could cultivate an intricate work of art out of seeds and dirt. 'Women born under the auspices of great happenings can handle anything. We can rise and walk about in our lot, wear it like every dress we ever bought that looked great but that we had no occasion for.'

And at the end of every day, as if to signal to the world she was off, she would pick a few stems in payment, using scissors to clip the flowers at just the right length. She would snip off the stamens and let their mustard dust fall down around her feet.

Inside the house, in a long glass cylinder half-filled with murky water, she would display the fresh ones, folding the old bunch in her hands of steel and taking them back down to the pile.

Crises weren't really her forté, my mother. It was the cycle of life she understood – growing things and then letting the dying ones go on the pile, draped in sunlight, with every edge, every lip, every leaf, curling in on itself.

Photo Credit: Sadie Coe

'The Queen's chain' was most recently published in **A Vase and a Vast Sea** (Escalator Press, 2020).

Anahera Gildea (Ngāti Tukorehe) is an essayist, poet, and short story writer. Her work has appeared in multiple journals and anthologies, and her first poetry book was published by Seraph Press in 2016. She is currently undertaking doctoral research focusing on Māori literature at Victoria University.

The Lake and the River

Elsie Locke

Garth held the boat steady for Tina to get in. She hesitated before stepping through the shallow water.

"Aren't you taking the transistor?" she said.

"No. I never do, on the lake," he replied.

Tina Maxwell pouted. She hardly ever went anywhere without pop music drumming in her ears, and she'd seen the transistor lying idle on the window ledge of the farmhouse where she'd come with her parents to spend the day. Garth was her cousin and they were both the same age, seventeen, but she didn't know him very well. His family had moved down from the north only recently to take up this farm. Garth was a strange one, Mrs Maxwell said; he didn't have much to say, but he was good with boats and he'd take her sailing.

"How dismal. There'll be nothing to listen to," said Tina.

"You can listen to the lake," said Garth.

"Has it got its own pop band?" she said, trying to make this sound like a joke.

"Wait and see. Or rather, wait and listen," was all he said.

The yacht was small and open, with room for only two, and the striped red-and-white sail looked too big for its body but performed well. The breeze blowing offshore took them quickly out onto the wide water in the bright sunshine. Garth wasn't talking. When Tina spoke to him he answered her questions only briefly. She had nothing to do but watch the shore receding, the shape of the trees round the house, and backdrop of the hills and gullies dark with bush. It was really quite beautiful. Tina loved to sketch: she must memorise the scene so that she could draw it tomorrow...

... and then she realised she was not only looking, she was listening; listening to the wind in the sails, the lake water chuckling past, two seagulls crying plaintively overhead.

A delighted smile puckered her face, and Garth noticed.

"Were you listening?" he asked.

"Yes, and looking too. Where are you heading?"

"The other side of the lake."

"All that far! Won't we be away too long?"

"I've got something over there to look at and it won't keep. If we get into trouble for being late back, don't worry, I'll take the flak."

Before long, the farthest shore became nearer. It was not very inviting; there were no tall trees standing out from the reeds and the flax. When they came ashore the ground was wet and their feet were squelching over marshy grasses. Clumps of rushes were scattered around like islands. Garth looked carefully into each one.

"What are you after?" said Tina.

"I can't remember which one it was," he answered.

Suddenly two birds rose noisily into the air and flew ahead, quite low, flashing their blue wings and trailing their long legs.

"Pūkeko!" cried Tina.

"Silly birds," said Garth. "They should know better than to give the show away."

He parted the next clump of rushes to reveal a nest shaped like a shallow bowl, and inside it a huddle of chicks clothed in black fuzz that stuck out stiffly, like fine wire, with outsize beaks poking upwards.

"So that's what they're like!" exclaimed Garth, all excited. "I hoped they'd be hatched by now."

He picked up one of the chicks and held it securely in his hand, laughing at its agitated piping.

"Is it all right to do that?" said Tina. "Won't you scare it to death, or chase its parents away or something?"

"I don't think so. Did you follow the films about how they saved the black robins on the Chatham Islands? They shifted them all over the place by hand."

"Yes, but the robins are an endangered species. They had to take risks to save them. Pūkeko aren't endangered, are they?"

"No more than other birds – or us for that matter. We're all endangered species, in a way. Go on, hold one."

Tina's chick wriggled and piped so shrilly that she nearly dropped it. "Oh, it tickles!" she said happily. "I've never held a baby bird like this before!"

"Worth coming to see, wasn't it?" said Garth.

Carefully they returned the chicks to their nest, squelched back to the shore and pointed the yacht for home.

"Weren't they cute, those chicks?" said Tina.

"Cute? They're incredible. When you think of the adult birds, how they stalk about like lords and ladies in their royal blue and crimson, and flicking their tails in that superior way – and this is how they begin, just balls of black fuzz."

Tina was astonished. The boys she knew never talked like this. They got steamed up about rugby and cricket, pop bands, cars and motorbikes, themselves and each other. Garth was a strange one all right.

She was going to ask what he meant when he said they were all endangered species in a way; but the gleam of the setting sun on the lake took the question out of her mind. It took longer to sail home because they had to tack against the wind, and navigate through the darkness by the lights of the farmhouse. The evening was warm and there was no possible danger, but when they pushed open the kitchen door, a storm of words broke over their heads: Tina's mother had just convinced herself that they must have been drowned in the lake.

But it was worth it, Tina told herself when at last she was home in bed, thinking of the lake and remembering the sound of the wind and the water and the seagulls crying overhead, and finding the nest in the rushes.

Next day at school, in her art lesson, she sketched the shoreline of the lake, and then the pūkeko chick in its wiry black fuzz and its outsize beak, nestling in her hand.

It was nearly the end of term and she thought it would be the end of school too; but it wasn't. All through the summer holidays, in between the beach and the tennis court, she looked for a job. She wanted to be a dress designer, or something else with an artistic side to it. There was nothing. Like so many others, she went back to school to fill in time.

The only lessons Tina took seriously now were in art, where her teacher said she was good, and her painting scenery for the drama presentations. She saw Garth occasionally when her parents had time to drive out to the farm by the lake; but he went to a distant high school, and he wasn't one of the bunch she spent her spare time with. And the yacht was taken out of the water for the winter, so they didn't go sailing again.

Because there were no examination goals for students like Tina who would leave school as soon as they had a job to go to, extra subjects were introduced. These included Peace Studies, which didn't excite Tina at all; it was too much like politics, which was usually rubbished in the Maxwell household. So when Miss Walters was going on and on in class about the effects of H-bombs, Tina switched off her attention. Her father always said it was never going to happen, the big chiefs were too scared of their own skins to let those things go bang. Her mother said they only made them because there was money in armaments and it kept the economies going.

Tina took out her sketch book and turned over the pages, Miss Walters' voice went rolling over her while she went through the reminders of autumn, winter, spring.

"What's that thing?" whispered the girl beside her.

"A pūkeko chick," she answered. And it all came back, the

nest, Garth telling her it was all right to pick up the chick and hold it –

And Miss Walters' voice broke through, saying birds!

"Remember this," she said. "It isn't only people we need to think of, it's the world web of life and the balance of nature. The insects would have the best chance of survival and the birds would have the least, so they're exposed –"

The horror of it broke over Tina's consciousness like surf breaking. She put her hand over the sketch, instinctively wanting to protect the helpless chick; then drew it away aware that this was futile. Those little birds, all burned up, stifled or slowly poisoned; and the seagulls overhead, the most exposed of all; the trees and the animals and the people – oh, it was monstrous, that anyone should leave even the slightest chink open, for such a disaster to happen!

Tears pricked at her eyes. Embarrassed, she clutched her sketchbook, muttered, "Excuse me," and rushed into the grounds and the shelter of a rhododendron bush where she could weep uncontrollably. Now she saw not only the chick but the adult birds flying with their long legs trailing, and heard Garth saying, "We're all endangered species, in a way."

What was the use of crying? It was all so hopeless. New Zealand wanted to keep out of the whole thing, being nuclear-free, but if the Northern Hemisphere blew up no place on earth could be isolated. Tina had taken in more of Miss Walters' information than she thought she had.

The buzzers sounded for morning break. At once the grounds were noisy with students talking, laughing, hassling one another, throwing balls about, taking practice shots at the netball goals. Tina bent her head and stayed where she was, hoping not to be noticed, but a girl slid onto the seat beside her.

"Why did you rush out like that?" she said. "What upset you?"

It was Olivia, not a special friend of Tina's, but a calm sort of girl who never picked on other people or got nasty. Silently, Tina showed her the sketchbook.

"Hey, you sure can draw!" Olivia said admiringly. "What a funny fellow. What is it?"

"A pūkeko chick."

"Is that right! But I can't believe you were crying over a pūkeko chick."

"Yes I was! Him and all the other birds and the animals and the people . . . what Miss Walters said, they could all be lost forever . . . I've never really thought about it before."

"You pushed it all away. Most people do."

"Dad says not to worry, it will never happen. So does Mum. They say nobody's so mad as to drop those bombs in earnest."

"Huh!" said Olivia. "They were mad enough to drop them on Hiroshima and Nagasaki, Bikini and Maralinga –"

"Maralinga, where's that?"

"Australian desert. They didn't clear out the Aborigines first."

"Didn't they? How horrific!"

"They hushed it up. They don't tell us what's really going on, ever."

"That's it then," said Tina. "It's all hopeless, we can't do a thing about it. This nuclear-free thing, old Lange thinks it's great, it's all right I suppose, but who takes notice of a little country like New Zealand?"

"Is that what your dad says?"

"Yes, why?"

"You quoted him before. I don't listen to my father. He's had half his life. We've got more to lose than they have."

"What is in it for us anyway? I can't see much ahead of me, not even a job. I wouldn't have come back to this stupid school if I could have found something."

"You haven't got that on your own. Me too – but I wasn't thinking about that. This nuclear thing: if it worries people here enough to get ourselves declared nuclear-free, mustn't it worry those people still more when they're near the action, like Europe and Russia and America?"

"I suppose so, but they can't do anything either."

"Oh Tina, you have got the miseries bad! Look, you ought to come with us on Friday night, I belong to a peace group –"

The buzzer sounded and the students began streaming back indoors. "I'll tell you about it later," said Olivia.

Friday night – and the Maxwells thought Tina was going shopping. Why tell them? She didn't feel up to any arguments or explanations. It was dark already, clear and cold. As she cycled towards Cathedral Square, Tina saw the first spring blossoms glowing pink in the light of the street lamps.

In front of the Cathedral a cluster of people was steadily growing. Banners were propped up saying NO MORE HIROSHIMAS, and STOP FRENCH NUCLEAR TEST, and FOR A NUCLEAR-FREE AND INDEPENDENT PACIFIC. Tina wandered through the crowd; all sorts were there, old and middling and young, and small children well wrapped up in their padded jackets and hoods. They were all friendly, but she couldn't find Olivia or anyone else she knew.

A woman stood on the Cathedral steps with a megaphone and made a speech to the passers-by. "Tonight we remind ourselves of Hiroshima and Nagasaki," she said, "when the atom bombs were dropped for the first time in deadly earnest. Hiroshima was about the same size as Christchurch here, it left a hundred thousand dead – "

"It finished the war, lady," shouted a man. "I know better than you, I was in the Islands then."

The Lake and the River

"It didn't finish anything!" said the woman. "It's what it started that counts. We remember those first victims so that it won't happen again. In Hiroshima they float lanterns on their river in memory of the dead. We have our own Avon River and it flows into the same ocean, the Pacific Ocean that links us together, and we're going to float lanterns too in solidarity with all who work for peace on earth –"

"Here they come! Make way!" came a voice.

"About time too, I'm freezing," said another.

A van edged its way through the crowd and stopped near where Tina was standing. Five people sprang out: the driver and his wife, a tall man with a beard, and Olivia, and – why, that was Garth! He disappeared quickly round the other side of the van, and then it was all action as the doors were opened and the lanterns were passed around.

They were simple home-made lanterns. Two pieces of wood placed cross-wise, a candle fixed in a holder at the centre, a surround of white paper to shield the flame from wind, and a wire handle. People were crowding in to make sure they didn't miss out. The children were eager, it was fun for them. Tina held back, not wishing to push in when she was new to all this – but here was Olivia saying, "Oh there you are Tina! Grab this one."

Guitars began to play and a woman sang into the microphone "Send the boats away", the song about the Peace

Squadron, the fleet of little boats that went out into the harbour to show the warships they weren't welcome with their nuclear missiles. "We did succeed about that, didn't we?" said Olivia. "The Government had to say No in the end." Then she was gone again.

When the song ended the call came to line up for the march to the river, and the candles were lit. It was a straggling sort of march with no military precision about it, just guitars and singing and big banners and small home-made signs and symbols.

People came out of the shops and lined the pavement, most of them silent, some shouting encouragement, and a few of them abusive. Tina felt oddly exposed, as if all eyes were on her alone, actually marching on the open street.

Garth appeared at her side. "I didn't expect to see you here," he said.

"I didn't expect to see you either. You could have knocked me down with a feather when I saw you get out of that van."

"Have you come on your own? What does my uncle say?"

"I didn't tell them I was coming. What about you?"

"They're all right. I came with a peace group from school."

"You never told me about that."

"You never gave me the chance."

They had come to the river, where the lawns made a gentle slope to the water. Voices were calling, "Garth, Garth! Over here, Garth!"

The Lake and the River

"Come and see my peace group," he said.

"I'll catch you up in a minute," said Tina, fiddling with her scarf and the buttons on her jacket.

But she didn't. She let Garth melt into the crowd so that she could take in the scene in her own way. It really was beautiful, with the street lamps shining through the tracery of the leafless branches of the trees, and making golden spotlights on the water. Men with long poles were helping the children launch their lanterns well out into the current. Tina stood back, waiting her turn.

"Can I take yours?" said the tall man with a beard who had come with the van. He was carrying a sort of hoe with three barbed hooks at the end.

"Could I do it myself?" said Tina. She wanted to say, "I've marched in front of those crowds and I want to finish it properly," but she didn't have to.

"Certainly," said Bill, giving her the tool.

She found a small space free of people, slipped the wire handle over one of the hooks, and stretched out the pole. The lantern wouldn't come off; she was afraid to shake it too hard in case it fell in upside down and doused the candle. "Give it a twist like this," said the man, showing her how. She tried again, the lantern slipped easily into the water and floated merrily away.

People were running along the riverbanks to follow their

lanterns, laughing and chattering. The children were having a wonderful time playing hidey and chasey around the trees. The candles twinkled across the twelve metre width of the river. Tina tried to keep her own lantern in view but soon lost it, and ran ahead to watch them pass under a bridge, squeezing a place for herself among the spectators. "Isn't it pretty?" they were saying.

A man stopped his car just long enough to ask, "What's all this about?" Nobody answered. I should have told him, thought Tina; and when another man, on foot this time, asked the same question, she was ready. "It's Hiroshima Day. They float lanterns in Hiroshima in memory of the people killed by the atom bomb."

"The Japs!" said the man. "Our enemies! You wouldn't know what they did to us, you weren't even born!"

"That bomb killed babies who hadn't done anything to anybody," she retorted.

This started quite a discussion, which quickly became political. Tina let them argue; she had said her piece and now she only wanted to look, to fix the scene in her mind so that she could capture it on paper tomorrow.

When the lanterns had nearly passed under the bridge she ran on, past the Town Hall with its fountains like glowing balls of dandelion fluff. The river flowed more slowly here and the lanterns kept getting stuck. One brave burly fellow plunged in up to his thighs, squealing comically at the cold, amid a barrage of shouts and jokes from his mates on the bank. The lanterns were released and floated on.

At last they had to be taken out, by order of the City Council which did not want the river littered with derelicts. Olivia appeared at Tina's side. "I've been trying to catch up with you," she said, "but people kept talking to me. Come on, I'll shout you a coffee."

Coffee! Marvellous. Oh, how cold it was! She hadn't realised before.

Olivia still carried a peace sign and the six or seven people in the coffee bar stared curiously. But soon the whole place filled up. The tall bearded man with the tool came in, and the burly one with his trousers well soaked – and Garth.

"How do you two know each other?" asked Olivia.

"We're cousins," said Tina. "It was Garth who found the pūkeko chick."

"Which got you here," said Olivia.

"How come?" said Garth, quite mystified.

"I made a sketch of that cute little chick, and Olivia saw it," said Tina, "and you'd said, We're all endangered species in a way – oh, I can't explain! But tonight we're reminding ourselves of something terrible that has happened and something worse that could happen, and yet it's been happy too! – and so beautiful; I didn't know our river could look so pretty. I'm going home to sketch how it all looked from the bridge. I can't explain that, either. Why should I feel happy?"

"You look prettier yourself now you've lost that helpless look," said Olivia.

'The Lake and the River' was most recently published in **takahē 100** (December 2020).

Elsie Locke (1912-2001) was a writer, a social historian, one of the pioneers of the New Zealand family planning movement, an activist for social justice, women's rights, environmental preservation, peace and civil rights. But she is best known as a writer for children. Her children's books and stories have been treasured by successive generations, and *The Runaway Settlers* (1965) has been continuously in print longer than any other New Zealand children's book. She also wrote copiously for adults: books, journalism, pamphlets and poetry.

Effigies of Family Christmas

Owen Marshall

There are to be eleven of them. Meredith, and Alun with his family, are the last to arrive. They pull over when the car has rattled past the cowstop. Alun and Meredith look across their father's land to the sea. Dry pasture, with sinuous movement only in those paddocks which have been shut up. A breeze from the sea: the land breeze is rare, a memory of the night. The beach between the land and the sea is an uneasy meeting place. It cants steeply, and the unstable shingle rattles back behind each wave. The brothers feel no need to comment on what they see, for superimposed upon it is their common experience. They have long before made any communication that mattered with this landscape. Alun lets his breath out in an eloquence which says, yes, here it is. 'Why are we stopping?' says Jane. It reminds her father to go on down the track towards the house.

The family appear on the verandah, come out on to the grass, when they see Alun's car. Mother has a thick apron over her dress. The apron has Pegs written on its broad, front pocket, but she uses it only in the kitchen. David's boy dances in front of the car. ' They're here. They're here. We can have our presents.'

'Presents after dinner, Rhys. You know that.'

Alun and Meredith see their father and Uncle Llewelyn behind the others, both with the same shy smile of reticence struggling with affection. Their father has his ankle-height slippers on despite the heat, and a pale, blue shirt that was bought to go with the best suit. 'Ah hah,' says Uncle Llewelyn during the greetings, 'Ah hah', and he smacks his hands together like two bricks, to show his relish in the family reunion. A light aircraft flies overhead, an intrusion on communal solitude. The family watch it pass; the sound comes back in the amphitheatre of the hills behind the house.

'Now we're all here,' says Mother, and she leads the way into the house. Meredith and David linger at the front door, touching the verandah supports as if they wish to reach out to each other. The unfamiliarity of brothers is a surprise to them.

'Nothing much changes, does it?' says Meredith. 'It's

stepping right back again.' David thinks his brother lives too far away, and has forgotten what things were like. Then he absorbs new things into the pattern of the old. 'Try me then,' says Meredith.

'The open hayshed wasn't built when you left.'

'It was. I remember collecting eggs in it. Several of the leghorns used to lay there.'

'No, that was the old stack. It wasn't even in the same place, but further back towards the yards. That hayshed wasn't built till you'd gone to Auckland.'

'It seems the same to me.'

'The farm's going back. I come over when I can, and Uncle Llewelyn still helps a lot. But Dad's not the farmer he was. There's hardly any cropping done at all now. All the fences need work. He still has sound stock though. I'll say that. Always good with stock, Dad was.'

'He hasn't the energy anymore, I suppose.'

'No.'

As they go through into the living room they can hear the excitement of Michael and Jane, helping Rhys put the presents beneath the tree. And they can smell the Christmas dinner. The fragrance is of this Christmas dinner, and all the others. There is a poignancy in the repetition. 'And you're not married yet,' says David.

'I've kept my freedom.'

'What's the matter with you? Deirdre, Meredith says that he dislikes women.'

'No, I didn't.'

'What girl would have him?' says Deirdre.

'I don't know why we married one of them each,' says Margaret. 'They've nothing to recommend them.'

'Just sheer effrontery caught us off guard,' says Deirdre.

'Animal magnetism. We all have it.' Meredith makes as if to kiss them both.

Uncle Llewelyn listens as he stands in the kitchen to enjoy the preparations for dinner. He marvels at the relaxed abuse, says 'Ah hah', smiles at the contestants in turn. Mother pushes on his back and he moves amiably out of the kitchen.

'I think we'll dish up,' she says to the other women.

Three roast geese, larded with bacon strips, and with a thyme stuffing. Bread sauce, peas, new potatoes, sweet corn, and salad as a concession to the heat. The sweat runs down the side of David's face as he eats. The quick sweat of a fit man. He opens the windows behind him, and the sound of the sea and the gulls comes louder to those of the family grown unaccustomed to the place. David, his parents and Uncle Llewelyn are no more aware of it that their own heartbeats. Rhys is rebuked for wanting to pull his cracker before it is time. 'Own geese, own bacon,' says Uncle Llewelyn on his brother's behalf. 'Everything but the corn.' Mother is moved to a further distribution.

'Meredith, you'll have some more peas and potatoes.'

'I couldn't, thanks.'

'Nonsense.' She spoons vigorously, as she would have done twenty-five years before. 'All our own, as your father says.'

His father's smile refuses credit for what he has achieved, and what he hasn't said.

Steamed pudding, with ten cent pieces smuggled in on the way from the kitchen to please the children. Pavlova, fruit salad and farm cream which is not whipped, yet so thick that it must be encouraged with a spoon. Some of the crackers don't explode, but all yield party hats, debased elephants and riddle sheets. Nuts, ginger, chocolate, and each adult pretending not to know what's black and white and read all over.

The heat and the occasion redden Mother's face; not her cheeks, but beneath her eyes, the side of her nose, and again along the chin line. Emotion in their mother takes a form of fierceness which they remember from their childhood. Margaret lets slip that Alun has bought her a car for Christmas. It's waiting for her in Sydney. 'I hope it brings happiness,' says his mother, and is angry for some time afterwards. She wants no glimpse of a way of life that is not her own. Alun is general manager designate for Australasia, but here Mother is determined he shall not outgrow the old relationships. 'Alun was always the complaining one,' she explains to the family. 'Always wanted something better than he had. I remember him moaning when he had to walk up to the school bus in winter. Neither of the other boys minded the same.' Alun smiles. He understands that every mother must punish a son who can succeed without her. Yet his mother's intensity surprises him. David is the favourite: he became a farmer like his father. None of them resent that, least of all David, who has the greatest cause. Being the favourite is a test of character. 'You were always difficult to please,' says Mother to Alun. 'Maybe Sydney will please you if your own country doesn't.'

The men sit on the verandah. They drink the beer which was not considered seemly at the table. Uncle Llewelyn is very much like his brother. His legs are too short for his heavy shoulders and forearms, and his face is lumpy and indistinct. Mother always says the brothers are typical of Welsh pudding-face working class. Uncle Llewelyn was his battalion's wrist wrestling champion in North Africa. He and his brother sit there, with green, crepe party hats above their lined, pudding faces. They confront the hills of the farm with composure, and add their presence although saying little. They are not accomplished with machines, and listen to David talking of the new seed drier. He is acknowledged to understand the voice of the motor. Yet with all his enthusiasm and youth, he has the gentleness of his father and uncle. A gentleness compounded to sadness perhaps. In many years the nature of it has eluded Alun and Meredith, yet on each return they recognise its presence. As the scent of ocean is never forgotten, yet impossible to convey without its presence.

'It's a nuisance to be growing old,' says Uncle Llewelyn. 'Do you know I can't sleep a night through now without a piss. I'm up for a piss every hour or two. And I find it difficult sometimes to swallow toast and bread. It gets stuck at the top of my chest.' The others laugh, and Uncle Llewelyn is not offended. It is accepted that a list of ailments will be mocked provided there's no immediate pain.

'A wife would cure everything,' says David. It is the best joke of the day.

The children have been waiting for the women to finish the dishes. They raise a cry for presents. 'Time for presents then, is it,' says Uncle Llewelyn, when Mother has given approval by her arrival. He carries Jane effortlessly to the lounge, the broad forearm a bench for her. The Christmas tree is a pine branch in a brass preserving pan, and the family presents are heaped around it. Mother allows the children to announce and deliver each in turn. It is the social ritual of which Confucius so approved. To Uncle Llewelyn from Meredith, to Alun and Margaret from Mum and Dad, to Uncle David from Michael, to Jane from Grandfather. Mother allows no distraction from the interlacing address to family members. Whatever the disparity of age or conviction, she will have it established that this is the family; this is the pledge to a continuity which cannot be disputed. This is the lineage of them all. To Mum from Deirdre; to Grandfather from Rhys. There is a lot of nodding and display; appraisals and thanks. The children wrench out their presents, but Mother picks at the sellotape, and folds the special paper with the future in mind. Jane cries because of the excitement, and because she hasn't a separate present for Uncle Llewelyn. Meredith gapes a little in the heat. He thinks of the beer still in the fridge.

It is the women's turn to rest, and the men's responsibility to take the children for a swim in the stock dam. David and Meredith carry bottles of beer and orange, to put in the water there. Michael is amazed by all the droppings, and Rhys, though younger, laughs at his ignorance of the country. 'But there's poop everywhere,' says Michael.

'A farm's mostly poop,' says Uncle Llewelyn. 'Poop and grass. Two forms of the same thing.'

'I don't like it,' says Jane.

Uncle Llewelyn is very gallant. 'Quite right. Ladies never do,' he says.

The ground of the gateways is worn bare by the passing of sheep, but, more than that, the earth itself is worn away, so that there is a dip which becomes a puddle in the winter. The gates drag even so, and are held by a collar of thick wire. The ends of the wire have been turned to a latch by the power of their father's hands.

The stock dam is large enough to keep the water clean. No one considers trusting the sea, for its undertow is a local legend. There remains a sense of irony, however, if only visual. For the group of them gather at the stock dam while the ocean stretches to the horizon. The three children squeal, and stir up the mud to make the water yellow. They smack with their hands, and splash the men on the bank.

'I stood on something.'

'Eels, eels,' they shout, enjoying the terror of their imagination.

'When do you leave for Australia?' David asks.

'I must be in Sydney in three weeks.' Alun lies on his side, propped on an elbow. He draws grass stems from their sheaths, and lances them into the pond. A flock of yellow heads sweeps by, bobbing like corks.

'Sometimes I feel I'd like a change myself. Living and dying where you were born isn't so wonderful a prospect.'

'It makes self-deception that much harder.' Alun plucks the grass, thinking of the way to continue. The wind blows his lank hair from one side of his face to the other. 'Change can sometimes seem a personal progress, when the essential journey bears no relation to distance at all.' Alun was able to talk of things that would make his family uneasy from any other source.

'Get your head right under, Michael,' calls Uncle Llewelyn. As he watches the children he shares their joy. He laughs when they do, his calls match theirs. He sits with his brother, a little apart from his nephews.

'I'd quite like to farm in Australia,' says David. 'I saw parts of Victoria that I could be happy in.'

'Imagine Mum and Dad if you went.' Wearing Joseph's coat has never been easy. The skuas gobble like turkeys, or give their keening cry, which hints at an essential hollowness of things.

Meredith, David and Alun watch their father. He has worn glasses for years, yet they are still an oddity. He puts them on awkwardly. The thin stems puzzle his fingers. The glasses are incongruous across his seamed, moon face. Glasses and hats don't suit their father. He has greater idiosyncrasies, with half a life of another way, and not even a letter since his parents died. Only Uncle Llewelyn can join in tacit reminiscence. Nothing is regretted it seems, but something sacrificed nevertheless for the new life. Alun points out to his brothers that their father never faces the sea when he rests. As a test they stand and talk to him, drawing him around to them. But soon he unthinkingly turns again, not right away from them, but so he can regard the downland, and the gully running up towards the road. He lifts his glasses, and rubs where they have rested. The Welsh are not great lovers of the sea in spite of all their coastline. Welsh men are miners, preachers, farmers and soldiers. Beneath the extravagance of song and poetry, an inward-looking people. Their father wasn't poet or singer, but he had a Celtic heart. His absurd glasses catch the sun, so that for an instant as his sons watch, the lenses silver over and his calm eyes are lost. His best blue shirt is open,, and the hair of his chest begins abruptly at the razor's edge, grey and so dense it hides the skin. Meredith moves to get more beer, and Uncle Llewelyn brings his brother's glass and his own. David tells the children to keep away from the top end of the dam where there might be snags. They have had enough. Rhys and Michael begin to quarrel over the one stick they have between them. Jane is thin, and as she comes from the deeper water her knee caps flick up and down as she shivers. 'Throw that stick away now, boys,' says Alun. 'We're going back to the house.'

'Let's all play cricket,' says Michael. 'We always play cricket on Christmas Day.'

Uncle Llewelyn is asleep on the verandah. His hands are as broad as they are long, and the folded skin of his brows almost hides his eyes. The dogs are not usually allowed within the house enclosure, but nothing is denied the children on Christmas Day. So sheepdogs play awkwardly at being pets. Jane has gathered Uncle Llewelyn's presents on his lap while he sleeps: tobacco pouch, patterned socks, petrol vouchers, handkerchiefs, cigars, parka, a box of twelve-gauge cartridges number five shot. There must be a good deal more to Uncle Llewelyn than such things represent, but it's not subject to easy scrutiny. If he is ever disappointed at being a supernumerary at his brother's Christmas, there is no sign of it. No outward show of affection either, yet they are rarely far apart. Every task on both farms which could not be done by one man, was accomplished by the two of them through the years.

Meredith stands for a time beside his mother, and they watch Alun and David play cricket with the children. Physical work hasn't yet stiffened David, and he is lithe and admirable. Alun has tapering, office legs. 'Soft as butter,' says his mother. 'The boy's as soft as butter.' There is an element of real contempt. 'And what does he want to go to Australia for, I'd like to know. We kept hearing how well he was doing in his job here.'

'It's a big job he's got over there. I don't think you realise just how much responsibility Alun has in his work. You'd be surprised, I think.'

'I blame Margaret as well. All these ideas. A car for herself, she said, and talk of a sauna bath in the house.'

'You know it's not Margaret. Things have always been different in the city; different tempo, other goals.'

'What Alun had wasn't good enough. He was always the discontented one.' She wouldn't relent. Any threat to old values and established patterns was received with bitterness. David must endure being favourite, Meredith being taken for granted, and Alun the guilt of finding his parents' life insufficient.

Tea is an attack again upon the food of midday, with the addition of ham, Christmas cake and strawberries. Daylight saving makes it only afternoon, and there are hours and hours for travelling, Mother says. She is reluctant to think of any member of the family leaving. For this one day in the year she can protect herself from the bare hills.

The bacon on the last goose has shaped itself to the breast, and Uncle Llewelyn makes a sandwich of it and thyme stuffing. 'Costs are beating us,' says Uncle Llewelyn. 'No matter what we do about production, the costs beat us every time. Most of the expenses we have no control over.' Uncle Llewelyn turns to his food again, and the pause is more than their mother can allow.

'Every union hanger-on in the country, every unnecessary middle-man and bureaucrat taking a fat living.' Her bitterness is unashamed. The family, each with an individual expression of wry restraint, carry on eating as she talks. Mother hasn't been educated to expect two sides to every situation, and the lifetime here hasn't suggested it.

'Workers in the city. . .' begins Margaret, but then she catches Alun's eye and falters. His mother carries on ready to start on the freezing workers, and her voice quickens in anticipation.

Michael puts strawberries into his mouth one after another. The sequence goes on and on. Uncle Llewelyn watches in admiration. David argues some point with his mother. 'Have you got the tree hut ready?' Meredith asks his mother. When he was ten David stole a fruit cake, and hid in the tree hut all night. No one had disturbed him, and the next morning he had returned for his breakfast, bringing the remains of the fruit cake as a token of submission. The children enjoy the story. David only grins and says he can't remember it. Each of the boys is the subject of some childhood anecdote, and the wives have learnt to join the laughter and the provocation.

Alun helps his mother sort the dishes to be washed. For a while they are alone by the window, and approach each other with a concern that always has the guise of exasperation. 'This job.' The manner in which she says it has a message in itself. 'This job of yours in Australia. Your father and I hoped that you'd be happy in Auckland.'

'The firm has its central office in Sydney. It's the

opportunity, you see. It won't come again.'

'I thought at least you might have considered your father. I thought your own country would satisfy you.'

'It wasn't easy. Margaret and I spent a lot of time talking it over.'

'But you're going nevertheless.' Each, with an effort, says no more about it, for it is Christmas Day. They work in silence until Deirdre comes back from collecting the best cutlery.

'Uncle Llewelyn and Michael are still eating,' she says.

The view is ever the same from the window above the bench. The blank wall of the garage, old when he was a boy, older now. The wood is swollen and distorted as rotten wood is. Successive coats of paint disguise the worst of it. At the corners the decay is complete, for there the water can get into the joints of the timber. He could put a fist right through it without pain. On the garage wall are the two safes for dog tucker, or game before it's dressed: gauze sides and simple wooden latches. The brown grass of the lawn ironed to the contours of the ground. The macrocarpa hedge with holes maintained in its denseness by nesting birds. The pipe-frame gate to keep out the hens and dogs, and a clean sack folded on the path before it. A pipe hammered into the garden, with the radio earth attached. And the dry bank beyond the macrocarpa, with the ice-plant like a wave mocking the drought. Behind it the pines, the downs, the persistence of the ocean's sound.

At the end of the day they are at the front of the house, and Meredith and Alun are wanting to leave. The children are still playing. 'Don't let the dog lick you, Michael. Never let a dog lick you,' says Mother. 'They've got germs you see, dear. In their mouths. Wash your face and hands, and use the hand towel.' Margaret begins to gather their things into the car. When Michael comes from washing, Alun tells his mother that they must leave. 'But you can stay the night. Of course you can stay the night. The children would love that.' She is sweeping them briskly along with her opinions, establishing any opposition to her views as selfish. Alun is surprised at the anger it raises within him. Anger not so much at her doing it, but at her assumption that he would not recognise it, that he and his brothers had not known and suffered it all their lives.

'We can't stay, Mother. I told you when we wrote. I'm sorry, but we must be away by eight, with the distance we've got before us.'

'Very well.' The red patches on her face flame.

Their father is baffled by the need to say goodbye. He shakes his head as he says the words. He puts a large hand on Michael's head, and then on Jane's. 'God bless now,' he says. The cadence of his youth has never been lost.

David comes with his brothers up to the turn-off. The three of them get out and stand together for the last time that day. 'I may have had my last Christmas here,' says Alun.

'Australia's not that far away.'

'It's not so much that. Mum's getting worse. All this compulsive manipulation of other people. We seem to have lost patience with each other. It's difficult for Margaret too.'

'That's why I've come this far with you, in a way. Not Margaret, but Mum, and what she's been trying to tell you both all day, and couldn't. The more difficult it was, the angrier she got.'

'About what?'

'Dad's going blind. One eye's all but had it now, and the other is just a matter of time. There's nothing can be done, they say, nothing can be done.' The brothers look down to avoid the glare of the setting sun. Margaret has no knowledge of what has been said. She leans across the car to the window.

'We should be starting, Alun.' He gives an odd gesture of dismissal and agreement.

'Is that the way of it then,' he says to David.

'We should go back down to them,' says Meredith.

'Not now. Not on Christmas Day. It'll only upset them both. Dad won't talk about it, even to me. Like everything else it's left to Mum. And this time she can't do it. For blindness she can't find a beginning.' David doesn't find it easy himself. So little is words, so much is feeling. 'I'll write to you,' he says, 'and I'll get Mum to write to you.'

Meredith and Alun watch him go back; his long shadow reaches down the track ahead of him. 'Poor Dad, poor Mum,' says Alun. 'She's been wanting to tell us all day. That's what it was. She couldn't do it.

'We could still go back.'

'Dad would know why. He wouldn't care for himself, but our knowledge of it is what he fears most. Christmas Day, and Dad's going blind, eh Merdy. There's a vision for you. Blind, calm Dad, and Mum keeping the world away from him. And there's nothing to be done, David says. You see that. Nothing can be done.'

They watch David almost at the house. The wind blows in from the sea as ever, and the seagulls cry our lives away on those long New Zealand beaches.

'Effigies of Family Christmas' was most recently published in **The Best of Owen Marshall's short stories** (Vintage Book, 1997).

Owen Marshall has written, or edited, over 35 books. Awards include the CNZ Writers' Fellowship, residencies at the universities of Canterbury, Otago and Massey, and the Katherine Mansfield Fellowship in Menton, France. His novel *Harlequin Rex* won the Montana New Zealand Book Awards Deutz Medal for Fiction in 2000. In that year he became an Officer of the New Zealand Order of Merit and in 2012 was made a Companion of the Order. He has received the Prime Minister's Award for Fiction and an honorary Litt D from Canterbury University, which in 2005 appointed him an adjunct professor.

Free as a Bird
David Hill

Except for a few sawing and nail-banging noises three or four fences away, the rest of the baches were empty. The boy Darrin liked the emptiness. At least today his mother wouldn't be at him to go and make friends with the other boys. On this glittering winter morning, the other boys were back in their home towns, at school.

He went down to the bank of springy kikuyu at the end of the bach's lawn in four jumps. Another two took him across the frontier of thinning grass where bank curved into beach. Three more, and he was over the creaking belt of driftwood and seaweed, bleached plastic bottles and orange twine that lay along the high-tide mark. He stopped to tug at one long stick where it poked out from a tangle of old fishing net, pushed it away when it refused to come, and went on across the grinding pebbles towards the rock pools.

Something was happening between his mother and his father. That was why they had all come to spend these four days at the McIntyres' bach; why he'd got nearly a week off school.

He'd heard his Auntie Diane talking to his mother about it. "At least see if a different environment makes you feel different. Try and get Lance to look at it from a different perspective." He didn't understand all she said; he knew he wasn't meant to, but it knocked displeasingly in his mind.

He'd gone down to the rock pools yesterday, on his first day at the bach. He didn't think much of them at first – the scoops and sink-sized hollows with their pitted rims seemed ordinary and unpromising. But they made him bend to look into them, then crouch to see past the surface glitter of sunlight. There were stones and glossy seaweed underwater; winkings of tiny claws beside the stones. A flicker of transparent tail as a cockabully betrayed itself above the matching bottom of sand. Only when he stood up and felt the cramp in his knees and the fronts of his thighs did he realise how much time had passed.

So, he came down eagerly to the pools this morning. More eagerly because he could feel the drag and crackle starting to build up, back inside the kitchen of the bach.

It was cold in the bach, too. He'd heard Mr McIntyre talking to his father. "Now there's no excuse for not being warm. You've got extra blankets in the wardrobe, and that little heater throws out a real glow." But his parents hadn't used the heater. They knew the McIntyres wouldn't accept any payment for the electricity, and they didn't believe in being in people's debt. He knew that before they went, his mother would make his father take the hand-mower out of the shed and do the lawns. She would sweep out both rooms, and wash the floors and windows. Even though nobody would be using the bach for another four months – he'd heard Mr McIntyre say so – they would leave it tidier than they'd found it.

Down at the pools, Darrin stood and blinked in the blue-and-yellow day. The winter sun was on his back. The sea breathed beyond the rocks. Gulls lifted up as he approached, and circled with their long cries above him.

He began making his picture come back, the picture he'd started on while he was down at the rock pools yesterday. In the picture, he was standing before his mother in some unspecified place and speaking to her. The words he was speaking weren't specified either, but his mother had her head lowered. Sentences were stepping from him which somehow raised his father to the status of wronged victim. Sometimes in the picture, his father came and stood beside him while he spoke and put a hand on his shoulder. But he didn't feel comfortable with that part.

Now he was looking at a seagull. The bits of his other picture went thin and slid away. One seagull, floating silent and tidy in a pool quite close to him. It hadn't flown up with the others. It just sat in the water; its head was still while its body trembled a little on the surface of the pool.

He began to move closer. Slowly, one step at a time. How near could he get before it took off? Near enough so it could see he was friendly? Near enough to touch it, even?

It was one of the small gulls. Grey feathers on its wings, a few black-tipped ones on its tail. He took another pace closer. The red beak ended in a little hook at the tip, where the top half fitted over. He'd never noticed that before. Another step. The eye was like little rubber rings, red on the outside, then white, red again, and black into the centre. Another step and another. The sun behind him.

The seagull was hurt. Along its breast and side, just above the water, exposed pinky-grey flesh glistened in the sunlight. It's torn its guts open on a rock or something, the boy told himself. He edged forward with one hand outstretched, making little noises of reassurance.

Then he was lurching backwards, away from the pool. The wound of pink-grey flesh had crawled and twisted along the seagull's side. The bird's body dipped in the water, then rose again. The beak opened, but made no sound. The eye stared. He saw the line of white suckers along the edge of the tentacle, where it gripped the bird.

One of his heels was dripping blood where he'd jarred it against the rock rim. He made himself go forward again, staring. Once more, as his shadow touched the water, the tentacle tightened and gleamed. Down under the big rock in the middle of the pool, the octopus braced itself against a new presence. The gull dipped with the movement. It might have been floating on a carefree swell. The dazzle of sun made it impossible to see down into the pool.

He knew straightaway that there was one thing he couldn't do. He couldn't put his hands on the tentacle, and try to pull it free. What if he touched the clinging limb? If the pink-grey flesh shifted sideways and came sliding over his fingers and wrists? His lips drew back at the thought.

A picture caught at him, and he was off across the rims of the pools, to the high-tide line of driftwood where the stick poked from its tangle of fishing-net. This time he didn't tug at the stick. He wrenched and tore till it came splintering away into his hands. He panted back towards the pool.

The bird was motionless again on the water. He knelt on the rock and stretched the stick's broken end out slowly till it touched the flesh of the tentacle. The white suckers wrinkled.

Next moment, he was lunging into the water beneath the

bird. Jabbing and threshing and hauling the stick from side to side in the pool. His own body and head were turned away, his eyes closed against what might come writhing up the stick at him.

The water frothed and slapped over the rock rim, and the gull lurched on sudden waves. Sand and mud rose from the bottom. The stick met a resistance like a wet sack. He snatched his hand away, and clutched it to him. Bird and stick floated side by side on the surface of the pool. A second tentacle had joined the first, glistening along the gull's white side.

He turned his back on the pool and ran for his father. Across the pebbles and up the bank of kikuyu grass to the bach. When he flung in through the back door, his mother and father were sitting silent at opposite ends of the kitchen table. In the darkness after the sun outside, he couldn't tell them apart at first.

His mother's voice began to say something about dirty feet, but he went straight over the top of her. It was like the picture he'd been making for himself earlier.

"Dad! Dad! There's a seagull down in the rock pools, and it's caught by an octopus! You've got to get it out. The octopus is gonna drown it! Please, Dad, you've got to come now!" Then he was off again, running before demands for explanation could snare and delay him.

Free as a Bird

When his father joined him at the pool, he was crouched again on the rim, trying to look down into the water. The man, who'd come striding jerkily down from the bach, said nothing to his son. Instead, he picked up the stick that was floating at the pool's edge and pointed uncertainly at the gull. And Darrin had another picture.

This one was from a month ago. Their cat had started choking on a fishbone. His father, who was nearest, had grabbed the animal and tried to pat its back. The cat twisted and squalled. His mother had said, "Give it here! God, you're useless!" With the animal tucked under her arm, she'd reached deftly with finger and thumb for the fishbone. His father had walked out of the room.

Now his father was jabbing with the stick in the water, just as the boy had done, only harder with his man's strength. The boy saw the same thing happen: the water lash and slop, the bird toss from side to side, the tentacles contract around it. But this time it was pulled deeper into the water, till its sides and folded wings were half-submerged. "Don't!" yelled the boy. "Don't! It's drowning!"

He knew instantly that they were the wrong words. His father's face went red and helpless. He slung the stick away so that it clattered and somersaulted across the rocks. Then he stooped and wrenched with both hands at a stone the boy couldn't even have moved. He rose, straddled above the pool, and lifted the stone high over his head.

"No, Dad! Don't kill it! No!"

The man stared at his son. He opened his mouth and his eyes as the seagull had done. Then he dropped the stone back on to the pool rim, and was striding, running back up towards the bach.

The boy stared after him, hands pressed against his ears where they'd jerked when his father scooped the stone high. He was heaving to breathe. His eyes felt tight and bulgy.

Then – "Dad! Dad! I know!" He too was off towards the bach once more. Blundering up through the kikuyu, reaching the top of the bank just in time to glimpse his father vanish inside the door.

He didn't go for the bach. Instead he snatched open the door of the shed where the lawnmower was stored. His hands scrabbled along the shelf for what he'd seen there yesterday – the pruning saw with its curve of rusty teeth.

He held the saw in front of him as he slid and stumbled back down to the pools. Both his feet were bleeding now from the pitted rocks. The seagull still floated silent on the surface of the water. The black centre of its eye stared at him.

Darrin stopped at the pool's edge. Then he drew back his lips again and stepped in.

The winter water gripped him up to his thighs. But it was only two steps into the middle of the pool. He did what he'd known he could never do, and seized the seagull with one hand. He reached beneath it with the pruning saw, and began hacking backwards and forwards with the hooked blade. He yelled as he sawed, and he felt the rusty teeth jag and tear. The tentacles gripping the bird contorted, then whipped away. The seagull was free in his hands.

He still whimpered and shrieked till he was out of the pool and headed towards the bach, the pruning saw dropped somewhere in the water. The gull held against his body with both hands. But he was silent except for the heave of his breathing by the time he reached the lawn at the top of the bank.

The seagull had lain unmoving against him all the way up from the rock pool. He would get it bread and a dish of water from the kitchen. Maybe there would be a tin of sardines his mother would let him open. But first the bird could rest where it was safe. He knelt down, and placed it gently on the soft grass of the lawn.

For a second, it sat as it had on the surface of the rock pool, body and eyes still. Then its beak opened for the second time, and stayed open. It shivered once along its length. A white membrane slid down over the eye nearest to him.

When Darrin finally stood up, his knees and thighs were stiff with cramp, the way they'd been yesterday after he'd knelt and stared into the life of the pools. He reached out with one foot, and gave the seagull a push. The bird sagged over on to its side. For the first time he could see its breast where the tentacles had gripped and crushed. The white feathers there looked just as unruffled as they did everywhere else.

He moved towards the bach in the glittering sunlight. His feet were covered with sand and blood. His jeans were soaked, and he'd ripped one of the cuffs of his jersey. He supposed he should wash his hands and feet under the outside tap, but he couldn't be bothered.

This time when he opened the back door, it seemed even darker inside than it had before. Once more his parents were sitting at opposite ends of the table, and he still couldn't make out at first who was which. They weren't looking at anything, and they weren't saying anything. As he looked at their faces staring past each other, he saw again the eyes of the seagull.

Photo Credit: Robert Cross,
Victoria University of Wellington

'Free as a Bird' was most recently published in **Hillsides - the best of David Hill** (Mallinson Rendel Publishers Limited, 2006).

David Hill lives in Taranaki, and has been a fulltime author for 40 years. He writes fiction and non-fiction for most age groups. His novels and stories for YA and younger readers have won various awards, and are published in some 15 countries and almost as many languages. His latest books are *Coast Watcher* (Penguin Random House NZ, 2021) and *Three Scoops* (One Tree House, 2021).

The Doll's House

Katherine Mansfield

When dear old Mrs Hay went back to town after staying with the Burnells she sent the children a doll's house. It was so big that the carter and Pat carried it into the courtyard, and there it stayed, propped up on two wooden boxes beside the feed-room door. No harm could come to it; it was summer. And perhaps the smell of paint would have gone off by the time it had to be taken in. For, really, the smell of paint coming from that doll's house ("Sweet of old Mrs Hay, of course; most sweet and generous!") – but the smell of paint was quite enough to make anyone seriously ill, in Aunt Beryl's opinion. Even before the sacking was taken off. And when it was . . .

There stood the doll's house, a dark, oily, spinach green,

picked out with bright yellow. Its two solid little chimneys, glued on to the roof, were painted red and white, and the door, gleaming with yellow varnish, was like a slab of toffee. Four windows, real windows, were divided into panes by a broad streak of green. There was actually a tiny porch, too, painted yellow, with big lumps of congealed paint hanging along the edge.

But perfect, perfect little house! Pat prised it open with his penknife, and the whole house front swung back, and – there you were, gazing at one and the same moment into the drawing-room and dining-room, the kitchen and two bedrooms. That is the way for a house to open! Why don't all houses open like that? How much more exciting than peering through the slit of a door into a mean little hall with a hat-stand and two umbrellas! That is – isn't it? – what you long to know about a house when you put your hand on the knocker. Perhaps it is the way God opens houses at the dead of night when He is taking a quiet turn with an angel . . .

"Oh-oh!" The Burnell children sounded as though they were in despair. It was too marvellous; it was too much for them. They had never seen anything like it in their lives. All the rooms were papered. There were pictures on the walls, painted on the paper, with gold frames complete. Red carpet covered all the floors except the kitchen; red plush chairs in the drawing-room, green in the dining-room; tables, beds with real bedclothes, a cradle, a stove, a dresser with tiny plates and one big jug. But what Kezia liked more than anything, what she liked frightfully, was the lamp. It stood in the middle of the dining-room table, an exquisite little amber lamp with a white globe. It was even filled all ready for lighting, though of course, you couldn't light it. But there was something inside that looked like oil and moved when you shook it.

The father and mother dolls, who sprawled very stiff as though they had fainted in the drawing-room, and their two little children asleep upstairs, were really too big for the doll's house. They didn't look as though they belonged. But the lamp was perfect. It seemed to smile at Kezia, to say, "I live here." The lamp was real.

The Burnell children could hardly walk to school fast enough the next morning. They burned to tell everybody, to describe to – well – to boast about their doll's house before the school-bell rang.

"I'm to tell," said Isabel, "because I'm the eldest. And you two can join in after. But I'm to tell first."

There was nothing to answer. Isabel was bossy, but she was always right, and Lottie and Kezia knew too well the powers that went with being the eldest. They brushed through the thick buttercups at the road edge and said nothing.

"And I'm to choose who's to come and see it first. Mother said I might."

For it had been arranged that while the doll's house stood in the courtyard they might ask the girls at school, two at a time, to come and look. Not to stay for tea, of course, or to come traipsing through the house. But just to stand quietly in the courtyard while Isabel pointed out the beauties, and Lottie and Kezia looked pleased . . .

***

But hurry as they might, by the time they had reached the tarred palings of the boys' playground the bell had begun to jangle. They only just had time to whip off their hats and fall into line before the roll was called. Never mind. Isabel tried to make up for it by looking very important and mysterious and by whispering behind her hand to the girls near her, "Got something to tell you at playtime."

Playtime came and Isabel was surrounded. The girls of her class nearly fought to put their arms round her, to walk away with her, to beam flatteringly, to be her special friend. She held quite a court under the huge pine trees at the side of the playground. Nudging, giggling together, the little girls pressed up close. And the only two who stayed outside the ring were the two who were always outside, the little Kelveys. They knew better than to come anywhere near the Burnells.

For the fact was, the school the Burnell children went to was not at all the kind of place their parents would have chosen if there had been any choice. But there was none. It was the only school for miles. And the consequence was all the children of the neighbourhood, the Judge's little girls, the doctor's daughters, the storekeeper's children, the milkman's, were forced to mix together. Not to speak of there being an equal number of rude, rough little boys as well. But the line had to be drawn somewhere. It was drawn at the Kelveys. Many of the children, including the Burnells, were not allowed even to speak to them. They walked past the Kelveys with their heads in the air, and as they set the fashion in all matters of behaviour, the Kelveys were shunned by everybody. Even the teacher had a special voice for them, and a special smile for the other children when Lil Kelvey came up to her desk with a bunch of dreadfully common-looking flowers.

They were the daughters of a spry, hard-working little washerwoman, who went about from house to house by the day. This was awful enough. But where was Mr Kelvey? Nobody knew for certain. But everybody said he was in prison. So they were the daughters of a washerwoman and a jailbird. Very nice company for other people's children! And they looked it. Why Mrs Kelvey made them so conspicuous was hard to understand. The truth was they were dressed in "bits" given to her by the people for whom she worked. Lil, for instance, who was a stout, plain child, with big freckles, came to school in a dress made from a green art-serge tablecloth of the Burnells', with red plush sleeves from the Logans' curtains. Her hat, perched on top of her high forehead, was a grown-up woman's hat, once the property of Miss Lecky, the postmistress. It was turned up at the back and trimmed with a large scarlet quill. What a little guy she looked! It was impossible not to laugh. And her little sister, our Else, wore a long white dress, rather like a nightgown, and a pair of little boy's boots. But whatever our Else wore she would have looked strange. She was a tiny wishbone of a child, with cropped hair and enormous solemn eyes - a little white owl. Nobody had ever seen her smile; she scarcely ever spoke. She went through life holding on to Lil, with a piece of Lil's skirt screwed up in her hand. Where Lil went, our Else followed. In the playground, on the road going to and from school, there was Lil marching in front and our Else holding on behind. Only when she wanted anything, or when she was out of breath, our Else gave Lil a tug, a twitch, and Lil stopped and turned round. The Kelveys never failed to understand each other.

Now they hovered at the edge; you couldn't stop them listening. When the little girls turned round and sneered, Lil, as usual, gave her silly, shamefaced smile, but our Else only looked.

And Isabel's voice, so very proud, went on telling. The

carpet made a great sensation, but so did the beds with real bedclothes, and the stove with an oven door.

When she finished Kezia broke in. "You've forgotten the lamp, Isabel."

"Oh yes," said Isabel, "and there's a teeny little lamp, all made of yellow glass, with a white globe that stands on the dining-room table. You couldn't tell it from a real one."

"The lamp's best of all," cried Kezia. She thought Isabel wasn't making half enough of the little lamp. But nobody paid any attention. Isabel was choosing the two who were to come back with them that afternoon and see it. She chose Emmie Cole and Lena Logan. But when the others knew they were all to have a chance, they couldn't be nice enough to Isabel. One by one they put their arms round Isabel's waist and walked her off. They had something to whisper to her, a secret. "Isabel's my friend."

Only the little Kelveys moved away forgotten; there was nothing more for them to hear.

Days passed, and as more children saw the doll's house, the fame of it spread. It became the one subject, the rage. The one question was, "Have you seen Burnells' doll's house? Oh, ain't it lovely!" "Haven't you seen it? Oh, I say!"

Even the dinner hour was given up to talking about it. The little girls sat under the pines eating their thick mutton sandwiches and big slabs of johnny cake spread with butter.

While always, as near as they could get, sat the Kelveys, our Else holding on to Lil, listening too, while they chewed their jam sandwiches out of a newspaper soaked with large red blobs.

"Mother," said Kezia, "can't I ask the Kelveys just once?"

"Certainly not, Kezia."

"But why not?"

"Run away, Kezia; you know quite well why not."

At last everybody has seen it except them. On that day the subject rather flagged. It was the dinner hour. The children stood together under the pine trees, and suddenly, as they looked at the Kelveys eating out of their paper, always by themselves, always listening, they wanted to be horrid to them. Emmie Cole started the whisper.

"Lil Kelvey's going to be a servant when she grows up."

"O-oh, how awful!" said Isabel Burnell, and she made eyes at Emmie.

Emmie swallowed in a very meaning way and nodded to Isabel as she'd seen her mother do on those occasions.

"It's true – it's true – it's true," she said.

Then Lena Logan's little eyes snapped. "Shall I ask her?" she whispered.

"Bet you don't," said Jessie May.

"Pooh, I'm not frightened," said Lena. Suddenly she gave a little squeal and danced in front of the other girls. "Watch!

The Doll's House

Watch me! Watch me now!" said Lena. And sliding, gliding, dragging one foot, giggling behind her hand, Lena went over to the Kelveys.

Lil looked up from her dinner. She wrapped the rest quickly away. Our Else stopped chewing. What was coming now?

"Is it true you're going to be a servant when you grow up, Lil Kelvey?" shrilled Lena.

Dead silence. But instead of answering, Lil only gave her silly, shamefaced smile. She didn't seem to mind the question at all. What a sell for Lena! The girls began to titter.

Lena couldn't stand that. She put her hands on her hips; she shot forward. "Yah, yer father's in prison!" she hissed spitefully.

This was such a marvellous thing to have said that the little girls rushed away in a body, deeply, deeply excited, wild with joy. Someone found a long rope, and they began skipping. And never did they skip so high, run in and out so fast, or do such daring things as on that morning.

In the afternoon Pat called for the Burnell children with the buggy and they drove home. There were visitors. Isabel and Lottie, who liked visitors, went upstairs to change to their pinafores. But Kezia thieved out at the back. Nobody was about; she began to swing on the big white gates of the courtyard. Presently, looking along the road, she saw two little dots. They grew bigger, they were coming towards her. Now she could see that one was in front and one close behind. Now she could see that they were the Kelveys. Kezia stopped swinging. She slipped off the gate as if she was going to run away. Then she hesitated. The Kelveys came nearer, and beside them walked their shadows, very long, stretching right across the road with their heads in the buttercups. Kezia clambered back on the gate; she had made up her mind; she swung out.

"Hullo," she said to the passing Kelveys.

They were so astounded that they stopped. Lil gave her silly smile. Our Else stared.

"You can come and see our doll's house if you want to," said Kezia, and she dragged her toe on the ground. But at that Lil turned red and shook her head quickly.

"Why not?" asked Kezia.

Lil gasped, and then said, "Your ma told our ma you wasn't to speak to us."

"Oh, well," said Kezia. She didn't know what to reply. "It doesn't matter. You can come and see our doll's house all the same. Come on. Nobody's looking."

But Lil shook her head still harder.

"Don't you want to?" asked Kezia.

Suddenly there was a twitch, a tug at Lil's skirt. She turned round. Our Else was looking at her with big, imploring eyes;

The Doll's House

she was frowning; she wanted to go. For a moment Lil looked at our Else very doubtfully. But then our Else twitched her skirt again. She started forward. Kezia led the way. Like two little stray cats they followed across the courtyard to where the doll's house stood.

"There is it," said Kezia.

There was a pause. Lil breathed loudly, almost snorted; our Else was still as stone.

"I'll open it for you," said Kezia kindly. She undid the hook and they looked inside.

"There's the drawing-room and the dining-room, and that's the –"

"Kezia!"

Oh, what a start they gave!

"Kezia!"

It was Aunt Beryl's voice. They turned round. At the back door stood Aunt Beryl, staring as if she couldn't believe what she saw.

"How dare you ask the little Kelveys into the courtyard!" said her cold, furious voice. "You know as well as I do, you're not allowed to talk to them. Run away, children, run away at once. And don't come back again," said Aunt Beryl. And she stepped into the yard and shooed them out as if they were chickens.

"Off you go immediately!" she called, cold and proud.

They did not need telling twice. Burning with shame, shrinking together, Lil huddling along like her mother, our Else dazed, somehow they crossed the big courtyard and squeezed through the white gate.

"Wicked, disobedient, little girl!" said Aunt Beryl bitterly to Kezia, and she slammed the doll's house too.

The afternoon had been awful. A letter had come from Willie Brent, a terrifying, threatening letter, saying if she did not meet him that evening in Pulman's Bush, he'd come to the front door and ask the reason why! But now that she had frightened those little rats of Kelveys and given Kezia a good scolding, her heart felt lighter. That ghastly pressure was gone. She went back to the house humming.

When the Kelveys were well out of sight of Burnells', they sat down to rest on a big red drainpipe by the side of the road. Lil's cheeks were still burning; she took off the hat with the quill and held it on her knee. Dreamily they looked over the hay paddocks, past the creek, to the group of wattles where Logan's cows stood waiting to be milked. What were their thoughts?

Presently our Else nudged up close to her sister. But now she had forgotten the cross lady. She put out a finger and stroked her sister's quill; she smiled her rare smile.

"I seen the little lamp," she said softly.

Then both were silent once more.

The Doll's House

'The Doll's House' was most recently published in **The Doves' Nest and other stories** (Century Hutchunson NZ Ltd, 1988).

Katherine Mansfield was a short-story writer, poet, critic, diarist and letter writer. She lived in Wellington, England and Europe where she died of tuberculosis in 1923. Her writing and status of a writer of merit is internationally recognised.

'The Doll's House' is thought to be drawn from Mansfield own childhood memories and the social dynamics of her small district school.

Letters from Whetu

Patricia Grace

English,
Room 12,
Period 1,
Friday.

Dear Lenny,

>Be like Whetu o te Moana,
>
>Beat Boredom,
>
>Write a Letter.

How slack finding myself the only one of the old gang in the sixth form. How slack and BORING. And it's so competitive around here – No chance of copying a bit of homework or sharing a few ideas. Everyone's after marks and grades coz that's what counts on ACCREDITING DAY and Nobody Never tells Nobody Nothing – No Way. ACCREDITING DAY – it's ages away yet everyone's in a panic. It's like we're all going to be sorted out for heaven or hell, or for DECIDING DAY, and I really don't know what it's all for. I've thought and thought but just don't get it. I tell yuh it just doesn't add up. Must tell you about DECIDING DAY inaminnit.

See . . . it seems we get put through this machine so that we can come out well-educated and so we can get interesting jobs. I think it's supposed to make us better than some other people - like our mothers and fathers for example, and some of our friends. And somehow it's supposed to make us happier and more FULFILLED. Well I dunno.

I quite like Fisher, I kind of appreciate her even though she thinks she, and she alone, got me through S.C last year, and even though she thinks I've got no brayne of my own. Little does she know that I often wish now that I'd fayled. How was I to know I'd be sitting here alone and so lonely learning boring things. Why do we learn such boring things? We learned boring things last year and now we're learning boring things again. I bet this letter's getting boring.

I sometimes do a bit of a stir with Fisher, like I say 'yous' instead of 'you" (pl.) It always sends her PURPLE. The other day I wrote it in my essay and she had a BLUE fit. She scratched it out in RED and wrote me a double underlined note – 'I have told you many times before that there is no such word as "yous" '(I wonder if it hurt her to write it). Please do not use (yous heh heh) it again.' So I wrote a triple underlined note underneath – ' How can I yous it if it does not exist?' Now that I think of it that's really slack – what lengths I go to, it's really pathetic. I mean she's OKAY, but I'm a bit sick of being her honourable statistic, her minority person MAKING IT.

I'll tell you something else, that lady sure does go on. And on. And on. She's trying to make us enjoy K.M. Kay Em is what she calls Katherine Mansfield, as though she and K.M. were best mates. Well I suppose Fisher could be just about old enough to have been a mate of K.M's . . . I'll tell you what she's doing. She's prancing about reading like she's gonna bust. Her lips are wobbling and popping, and she's sort of poised like an old ballet dancer. She does a couple of tip-toes now and again. Sometimes she flaps the book about and makes circles in the air with it. I don't think she'll burst into tears.

Do you know what? When she waves and flaps the book about she doesn't stop 'reading', so I suppose that she means she knows her K.M. off by heart, bless her HART (Halt All Racist Tours) , punctuation and all. I don't think her glasses will quite fall off – Beat Boredom, wait and hope for Fisher's glasses to fall off and cut her feet to ribbons.

Gee I enjoyed our day at the beach last weekend, and us being all together again first time for ages. Andy looks great. All those hours in the sea and those big waves lopping over us. Hey why don't we save up and get us a surfboard?

I got my beans when I got home though, boy did I get my beans. Yes, and we'll take some food next time, and some togs and towels (to save our jeans from getting so clean). What about this weekend, but we'd have to contact Andy. Anyhows think on it. Really neat. It wuz tanfastic bowling around in those breakers hour after hour.

And what about those new songs we made up – haven't done that since fourth form. Soon as I got home, after having my ears laid back by Mum and Dad, I went and wrote that second song down so we wouldn't forget it. I like it, I really do. I'm writing out a copy for each of us and I'm sending Andy's with his letter which I'll write period 4. I'm writing letters to all of you today. Gonna post them too, even though I see you all at lunchtime (except Andy).

Can't remember the words to that first song, there must've been about twenty verses, and what rubbish. I can remember the 'Shake-a Shake-a' and the 'Culley bubba' bits, and I remember Iosefa's verse,

Tasi lua tolu fa
Come a me a hugga, hugga
Shake-a Shake-a Shake-a

Culley bubba longa-a long-a.

And

Tangaroa Tangaroa
Little fish belong-a he a,
Shake-a Shake-a . . .

Then there was another one about a shitting seagull – well never mind. Great music you and Andy made for it though, and only the waves to hear.

She's still flapping, and poncing, and I swear there's a tear in her eye.

And yes. I said I was going to tell you about DECIDING DAY. Went to the library on Monday, and opened a book which I started reading in the middle somewhere. Well this story is all set in New Zealand in the future ay, and there's been a world war and wide devastation.

There are too many people and they're short of stuff – goods, manure, natural resources and all that, so it's been agreed that all the cripples, mentals, wrinklies and sickies have to be sorted out and killed, then recycled. DECIDING DAY is the day the computer comes up with who's human and who's 'animal'. They're going to make them (the dead mentals, etc.) into energy, and use their skins for purses, etc. The kid down the road becomes your new knife handles, buy a bottle of drink and it's your granny stoppered inside ready to fizz. Turn on your light and there's your nutty uncle.

After that there'll be a perfect society and a life of ease so they reckon. Neat story?

After DECIDING DAY the fires are going for weeks and weeks, and there's smoke and stink everywhere. The remaining people (not very many coz the computer doesn't find too many 'humans') try to make out they can handle it, but they can't. They can't hack it at all, and they want to chunder over and over, or fall about mad screaming.

Well e hoa. Fisher's winding down, and period one almost over. Love talking to you, not bored at all. See you lunchtime but you won't get this til next week. Gonna get me some envelopes and stamps and do some lickin'.

Arohanui,

Whetu o te Moana.

(I was named after a church.)

Letters from Whetu

Mathematics,
Room 68,
Period 2,
Friday.

Dear Ani,

The new maths teacher is really strange. He never calls the roll but just barges in, goes straight to the rolling blackboard and starts writing. At the same time as he's writing he's mumbling into his whiskers and flinging the board up. His face is only about six inches from the board and you keep thinking he might catch his nose in it. I think he's half blind.

When he gets to the end of the rolling board he starts rubbing out with his left hand and keeps on scribbling his columns and numbers with his right. At the same time he keeps up his muttering and his peering. All he needs now is a foot drum and some side cymbals. When the bell goes he turns round as if he's just noticed us, his specs are all white and chalky and his whiskers are snowy, and he has a tiny pyramid of chalk pinched between his finger and thumb, all that's left of a whole stick. What a weird-o. Then he yells out page numbers and exercise numbers for homework and says, 'Out you go. Quickly.' As we go out he's cleaning his bi-fokes and getting out a new piece of chalk ready for the next lot of suckers. No wonder I'm no good at maths (not like Lenny who's got a mthmtcl brayne. What say we save up for a srfbrd and Lenny can be the treasurer).

Trust you to get stuck halfway up the cliff. Hey I got really scared looking at you, then I got wild with the boys just leaving you there and doing all that Juliet stuff with the guitar. Wasn't til I started up to help you that they decided to come up, and even so they were only assing around.

Then it was really beautiful up on that ledge after all. Wasn't it? You forget, living here. Living here you never really see the sun go down, or you don't think of it as being anything really good. Sometimes if you're outside picking up the newspaper or the milk bottles you see the sky looking a bit pink, or else it just gets dark and you know it's happened. But you don't think 'The sun's going down,' you only think 'It's getting dark.' Mostly we have the curtains over the windows because of people going past, and you think they might LOOK IN, or something TERRIBLE like that. And what if one of them HAD A GUN and aimed it at you? What if there was a loud bang, and a little hole in the window the size of a peanut, and a big one in your head the size of an orange? What a splash of colour, what a sunset and a half that would be. Yes and anyway we need the curtains over the windows because of the telly being on. Telly is a sort of window too, with everything always on the other side of the glass. After a while you don't know the difference between 'looking out' and 'looking in'. Well you know what I mean fren, you don't ever think how it is sitting halfway up a cliff making up songs, with the sun dropping behind an island.

You weren't scared anymore once we all got up there, and the sun settled at the head of the island like a big bloodshot eye just for a sec. Then it dropped behind like a trick ball.

You don't ever think of the sky slapped all over red and orange, and the sea smothered in gold-pink curls. When you think back you can see it all again, but can't quite feel the same, like your skin is stretching tight over your body, like your eyes are just holes and it's all pouring in.

Well what a climb down in the dark, then the hunt in the dark for shoes. If we hadn't had to look for our shoes we'd have caught an earlier train home. God I got my beans when I got home. Then of course there was that long wait in the greasy shop for our greasies. I was starving.

When we were little we always used to go to the beach – every low tide even in the cold weather. But now that us kids have grown up I don't think Dad likes it anymore. Anyway he's so busy and on so many committees – marae committee, P.T.A., Tu Tangata, District Council – and Mum's almost as bad. We're never home together these days, especially now that Hepa's flatting and Amiria's married. As for Koro, he's never in one place for a day. He gets called north south east west, if not to a tangi then to a land meeting, if not to a land meeting then to a convention. Well it's no wonder we never get to the beach or see each other much.

Er um! Hepa turned up on Saturday, so Dad went and got Amiria and John. Er! Koro was back from Auckland, so, er, I was the only one not home. And NOBODY knew where I was. Tricky huh? Well we didn't know we were going to the beach did we? We started out to meet beautiful Andy off the train and ended up getting the train north.

Hey old chalk-chewer is yelling out page numbers, he's remembered we're here. He looks like a sort of constipated old Santa – I'd better end this letter inaminnit.

Yes Dad cracked a fit and I took a bit of flak from Mum as well. They were all dressed to go out and they'd been waiting hours for me. Of course what Dad really thought was that I was out getting myself popped, it's what they all think but won't say. Ding Dong. Got to bed midnight. Or was that the time we got home, heh heh?

The beach. It beats late shopping nights by a long way. Gotta go. I'm the only one left, goodbye fren. Writing to Iosefa next period. See you lunchtime, but you won't get this til next week.

Much love,
Yours ake, ake, ake,
Star.
(I'm a Star
I'm a Star
I'm a Monstar.)

Letters from Whetu

Geography,
Room 3,
Period 3,
Friday.

Dear Sef,

I write to you amid a shower of topographical maps, aerial photos, fault lines and air masses. What a circus. Lattimer arrives loaded with books which he bangs on to a table. Then he starts spouting – So you SEE, So you SEE – producing his cross-sections, graphs, map keys, land formations like tricks out of a hat. After a while he bounces round the room dealing out worksheets and slamming books down in front of us, creating his own earthquakes.

Writing to Ani I remembered how we always used to go downtown on late shopping nights. She and I used to make all sorts of excuses so we'd be allowed to go, and so did you. You used to tell your mother you were going on a training run, then you'd run into town and we'd all meet and spend our money on take-aways and junk. Then we'd hang round the fountain with the other kids and hope a fight might start up between our college and the one up the line. We always knew who was out to get who, and who was ripping off what from where. The night we caught the taxi home (with Lenny's money) you had to run up and down the road to get puffed and sweaty before you went inside. I got home wet from you throwing half the fountain on me. We'd all swapped clothes as usual.

Well parents get upset about funny things. Wasn't allowed downtown for ages and ages and used to feel really slacked off on late-shopping-nite-nites because I wanted to be out there having FUN, that was winter. Hey what babies we were, running round, hiding in doorways and hoping all the time that something really awful would happen.

Yes Lattimer's got a great act there. Maybe we should all crouch on our desks like circus tigers and spring from table to table and roar, and swipe the air with our paws.

What about the time we took your little cousins to the zoo, and Andy got smart to the ape and it went haywire. Then Andy walked away whistling and looking at the sky. Remember the ducks zooming in, and the tiger that turned its bum round at feed time and pissed on the people. And Ani pissed herself laughing. Oh Ani, what a roly-poly, what a ball. Ani's really neat.

Well the ape was bouncing all over its cage with its big open mouth as pink as undercoat paint, baring his old smoker's teeth and trying to wrench the bars apart. Then he began snatching and grabbing at his own arm, his own shoulder, his own head, and at the same time he kept opening his mouth and slamming it shut, and putting his bottom teeth almost up his nose. His eyes were as black as print and glinting like flicked pins.

Our mate Lenny looked at the ape and said, 'Honey baby come to my pipi farm and I'll give you a gink at my muscles.' Spare It! Poor monkey, with its thumbs on back to front. The palms of its hands looked like cow turds.

I really wonder about Lattimer. The way he throws himself about the room you'd think he was really trying to knock the walls down and make a run for it, or perhaps he wants to give himself a crack on the head so he can be pulled out by the feet.

Anyway he's all right – busts out in a sick grin every so often. Remember Harris (harass) and her screwed-up face, and how she used to walk in and shove open all the windows because we all stank. I really wanted to walk out that time Andy left, if only I'd had the guts. Everytime she got on to him I felt like dying, even before I knew Andy properly. She'd never believe what Andy's really like, she was just so scared of him, of his looks, of the way he talks, of his poor clothes. Most of all she must have realised Andy had her taped, over and over, although he never said anything. On that last day I reckon it was his quietness and his acceptance that got to her. She was screwed up with hate, and screaming. Writing to Andy next period and won't forget to tell him about Palmer's DISGUISE.

Sometimes I can't hack the thought that I didn't follow Andy down the road that day, instead of sitting here waiting to 'realise' my 'potential'. Hey Sef, when and how does potential become whatever it's meant to become? I mean Mum and Dad have all these IDEAS, they're both getting their THRILLS over my education and I reckon I'll be sitting behind a desk FOREVER.

Funny though, if it had been either one of them they'd have gone out the door with Andy without thinking twice, because they really know what's important. It's only me they've got under glass. Anyhows I'll leave it before I start thinking what a sucker I am.

And now I'll talk about the beach. Nex' time we'll take all our gears, especially FOOD. If you're wrkng next wknd, or if Ani's wrkng, or if Andy can't come, we'll go another time. Soon. But gee Sef, the dropping sun and the bleeding sky and those great fat humping seas, the seagulls . . .

I often dream about flying, and sometimes in the dream I'm afraid of what I'm doing, and other times I'm so happy and free flying about, up above everyone and everything, going anywhere I want . . . If I wasn't me I'd be a seagull belting out over the sea and throwing myself at any storm, ANY STORM. What would you be, e hoa, if you weren't you?

Gotta go Iosefa, he's snapping up all his books and hand-outs, and now, slurp, they'll all back in the trick box. Howzat? See ya lunchtime, which is now.

    Much love from
    Star of the Sea.

Letters from Whetu

History,
Room 42,
Period 4,
Friday.

Dear Andy,

Great to see you on Sunday, you and your old guitar. I hardly remember going to the beach, only being there. When we came to meet you off the train we didn't quite expect to find ourselves on the next one heading north. Suddenly we were off the train again and legging it to the beach all those miles. But it seemed no distance, the road just rolled away under us and only our talking tongues were in a sweat. Hey, that neat car, 'You got the Mercedes, I got the Benz' (according to Len). I've been writing letters all morning as part of my anti-boredom campaign.

What I want to tell you is that Iosefa has got a black eye. On Tuesday, Palmer, who is the new VICE principal, disguised himself (as a flasher) and pounced on Lenny, Iosefa and some other boys who were all puffing up large on the bank by the top field. True. He put on his old raincoat, ankle length no less (a real flasher's job), and one of those work caps that have advertisements printed on them – Marple Paints. The boys thought it was a member of the public taking a short-cut to the road so didn't take much notice. Instead it was old P. ready to pounce, wearing his usual greaser's grin.

All the letters went home to parents as usual —

'Dear   , I wish to bring to your notice that your son/daughter   was discovered (!!!) smoking in the school grounds on   (date, etc...etc.).

Iosefa got thumped by his old man, and Lenny's mum screwed up the letter and laughed her wrinkled old head off. On Wednesday, Palmer's blackboard was covered with compliments — 'Palmer's a wanker' and all the usual things. Someone drew a spy glass with a gory eye looking through. And you know Rick Ossler? His old man came up and shook 'the letter' in Palmer's face and called him a Creeping Jesus. Well I laughed and laughed. Never heard that expression before, but when I told Mum she said it was an oldie.

Anyway enough of that. Neat fun sitting up on that ledge singing up large, we must've been there for hours. Every now and then I'd think of all our mates from fourth form days, and how we'd all go over to D6 and sing and act like fools, and make up funny songs.

But Angie and Brian, Willy, Judy, Vasa, Hariata, lots of others . . . I was thinking too of how we all used to terrorise the town on late-shopping-nite-nites. Wonder what they're all doing now?

Before I went to bed on Saturday (and after I'd had my ears blasted for being back late), I wrote down the words of our song so we wouldn't forget them. It seems there are things to know about our songs, even the rubbish ones, things we don't really know yet. There are so many things to know, and I really envy you because you're learning some of them. I want to know important things, and also I want to know what's important.

Slitting the throat of a sheep and hanging it up kicking seems to be a real thing, like picking watercress, and even though it's something you can do and I can't, I still want to know about it. Even though I wouldn't want to cut the belly and haul the guts out I know it must sometimes be all right to have blood on your hands. Or if not blood then dirt, or shit – on the outside where you can see it. You see I've got this bad idea that I'm sitting here storing all the muck up inside me, getting slowly but surely shit ridden. As for you, you've never held any shit, ever, and never will.

But other things, so many things, I mean, I want to know what goes on in houses, especially in houses on hills with trees round them. What do the people there say to each other? What do they laugh about and what do they eat? Are their heads different from them being up higher? Do they chew gum, how can I know?

Are girls who work in clothes shops just like me, or do their faces fall away when night comes, and does someone hang them limp on a rack until morning? Does central heating dry people out and make them unable to face the weather? Well I could go on and on.

E hoa. I want to walk all over the world but how do I

develop the skills for it sitting in a plastic bag fastened with a wire-threaded paper twist to keep the contents airtight. You sit cramped in there, with your head bowed, knees jack-knifed up under your chin.

If I walked round the world I'd wear two holes in my face in place of eyes and let everything pour in. I reckon I could play an alpine horn.

The other day two fifth formers bought pot from the caretaker then potted him. And a lot of fourth formers are getting high from sniffing cleaner fluid which they pour on their sleeves. Peter got his arm blown up when his mate lit a cigarette, and now he's in hospital (luckily). Were we that suicidal two years ago, screaming round town in our jackets wishing to see someone slit from eye to knee with a knife?

I saw a girl nick a bottle of the stuff from a stand in McKenzies yesterday but I didn't do anything. There were two rows of it on a glass shelf at 89c a bottle.

And now the bell rings and we're almost through the day. No more letters to write, but next period (last one) I'll write out THE SONG for everyone (see yours below). If I write slow enough it might use up the hour.

Well dear friend, write back straight away and tell us when you can come down again. WE'VE GOT PLANS and WE SEND OUR LOVE.

      Yours 4 eva,
      Whetu.

Sky love earth
Shine light
Fall rai-ai-ain.
Earth give life
Turn breast
To chi-i-ild.

Child
Steal light
Turn away rai-ai-ain.
Thrust bright
Sword
Deep into ea-ea-earth.

Mother bleed
Your child
Die.
Bleed mother
Child
Already dead.

W – o – te –M.

'Letters from Whetu' was first published in **The Dream Sleepers and other stories** (Longman Paul, 1980).

Patricia Grace is one of New Zealand's most celebrated writers. She has published seven novels and seven short-story collections, as well as a number of books for children and works of non-fiction including her recent memoir *From the Centre*. Patricia has won numerous awards for her books including *Potiki*, *Dogside Story* and her children's story *The Kuia and the Spider*. Patricia was born in Wellington and lives in Plimmerton on ancestral land, in close proximity to her home marae at Hongoeka Bay.

A Good Boy

Frank Sargeson

I never wanted to be a good boy. I've got myself into a mess I know, but won't anyone ever understand that? Mother always said, If you take *my* advice you'll always be a good boy. How could I tell her I didn't want to be a good boy?

I was always real sorry for mother and father. They didn't seem to have any pleasure in life. Father never went out after he'd come home from work. He just sat and read the paper. His stomach was bad too, and made noises, and he kept on saying, Pardon. It used to get on my nerves. I used to watch him and mother when I was supposed to be doing my homework. Sometimes the look on mother's face gave me the idea that inside she wasn't properly happy and was wanting pleasure just the same as I was. It used to make me come over all sentimental and I'd have a job to keep myself from crying. She used to say she never had a minute's rest, and she'd keep on darning socks or something like that right until it was bedtime and she had to go and make father's cocoa. They were good people, both of them. And they expected me to be good too. And how could I tell them that I didn't want to be good?

I couldn't tell them. Instead I pretty often played the wag instead of going to Sunday school and did things like that and they never found out. And when I started going to that billiard saloon I kept that dark too, because father and mother would never have stood for it. It was when I'd left school and could only get odd jobs, and father was making me swot at book-keeping so I could be an accountant instead of just a dry-cleaner like him.

Gee, but I used to have some fun in that billiard saloon. Paddy Evans kept it. He'd been a jockey but he'd pulled a horse and got disqualified. They said it was a crook business right through like they say all racing is. The trainer of the horse and the owner and a bookie were all mixed up in it. You know, crossing and double-crossing each other, but it was Paddy who got it in the neck. Anyhow Paddy was a good sort, even though he did have the hardest dial you ever saw on a man. And so was his wife a good sort too. Of course they weren't good people like father and mother, they never went to church or anything like that, and it's a fact that Paddy ran a book, but they were real good fun. I'll tell you how fat Mrs Evans was. She was so fat she always had to make a split in the top part of her shoes and sew in a little gusset. She was absolutely full of fun, made a joke out of everything, and wintertimes when it was time to close she'd nearly always bring out coffee and toast.

You know I could never see anything much wrong in the billiard saloon. Most of the boys never had enough money to put anything on with Paddy, and billiards is a good game. It takes a boy's mind off thinking too much about cuddling girls and other things. And with all those angles to think about it's as hard as trying to work out one of those geometry theorems. Me and the boys were all good cobbers too. They were nearly all boys who worked in shops and motor places, and they used to ask me things like what it means when you put & Coy. on a cheque, and they used to sling off at me when I couldn't tell them. Well, I don't believe even a bank-manager can say why you put & Coy. on a cheque. Not properly say. But later on it was like I've said, I was just one of the boys. They didn't sling off at me and we were all good cobbers.

Well, of course father found out. I was a bit too big then for him to give me one of those hidings but gee, the way he and mother talked at me was like nothing on earth. For peace and quietness I had to promise I wouldn't go to Paddy's place any more. Father had his knife into Paddy properly. He stuck him up in the street and roused him up hill and down dale, and one day when he happened to see him riding his bike on the footpath he had him fetched up in Court. Oh, hang it all, I didn't blame father. He and mother are both good people, you can't deny it. But it wouldn't have done any good telling them it's no use trying to make people good if they don't want to be good.

Another thing, I'd have done anything to please mother at that time because it was just before my little sister was born. I'd noticed it was going to happen, and it sort of got under my skin because there'd been only just the three of us in our family ever since I could remember. At any rate, when it did happen it was lucky for me because it gave father and mother someone else to think about and made it easier for me to get out at night and see the girl that I've landed myself in this mess over. She worked in a restaurant and gee, it was fun to sneak round the back and help her wash the dishes.

Oh hell, what's the use of going on? I thought while they're keeping me here in clink I'd write the story of my life, then perhaps if my little sister reads it when she's grown up *she* might understand that I never wanted to be a good boy. But it's all no good. What I've written so far is all balled up and doesn't explain what I want it to at all. All I want to explain is that I never wanted to be a good boy, and how can I explain that?

I killed that girl. Yes. It was because she cracked on that I was the only fellow she was going with but I found her out. And what did I do? Did I remember that I never had been a good boy, and never wanted to be a good boy? Did I remember how the boys said Paddy Evans' wife used to go out with a lawyer who bought her a fur coat, and Paddy just said he wished he'd buy her a muff as well? Did I? No I didn't. I went all righteous just like father and mother used to go when they caught me or anyone else playing *them* a dirty trick. Gosh, when I killed the girl I felt better and cleaner than I've ever felt in my life. I bet father used to feel just the same as I did then when he used to give me those hidings. I never wanted to be a good boy, but when it came to a sort of test I found I was a good boy after all. I did the right thing. I've told the detectives and the lawyers and the doctors and everybody that over and over again, and they won't believe me. You'd almost believe they think I'm off my block which is just plum ridiculous. I've told them I've never been a good boy, all except that one time when I did the right thing just like father and mother had always tried to teach me. That was the time I killed the girl.

Oh Christ, won't anyone ever understand? I'm all balled up, I know, but I'm trying to explain. I never wanted to be a good boy.

Photo Credit: John Reece Cole, 1964

'A Good Boy' was most recently published in **Frank Sargeson's Stories** (Cape Catley, 2010), and first published in the collection, **A Man and His Wife,** (Caxton Press, 1940).

Frank Sargeson was influential not only through his writing, but also as a friend and mentor to other writers. Described as one of New Zealand's greatest literary innovators and mentor to the literary community, Frank Sargeson was a novelist and short story writer who became internationally known as the pioneer who broke from colonial literary traditions to an idiom that expressed the rhythms of New Zealand speech and experience. He qualified as a lawyer before committing himself to full-time writing.

Days of Our Lives
J.P. Pomare

After school I stop by the drain where we found the arm. It starts beside the cage for unwanted calves and ends at the ditch cutting along the perimeter of McGregor's farm. The day of the arm, when the tar became soft and sticky and we were giddy with the coming summer break, we had crawled through it. Jack first then me.

I think enough time has passed, I'm ready to crawl through it again. I put my schoolbag before me, drop down to the grass on hands and knees and I enter the drainpipe. The concrete is hard on my palms and shins and it gets harder the deeper I crawl. The end is a bright circle, pickle green grass, flattened where the water normally runs. I turn my elbows in against my body. Dad once said, rats can compress their bodies to the size of their head, so if they can get their head in they can get their body in. I think if I really needed to, I could make myself smaller, I could draw my bones, organs, limbs into myself. He had said that when we found the rat, its back snapped with only a coppery spot of blood on the wooden trap. He had lifted it by the tail and dropped its stiff body in the rubbish bag then smeared his hand down the outside of his thigh and grinned at me.

There's something soothing about being at the centre of the drainpipe. I lay there still in the darkness for a moment, just listening to the sounds. When I say hello the word bounces around me. A car passes on the road above. It's all drumming and paint rollers, then no sound at all. I remember the fly landing on my face when I was last in the drainpipe; all I could do was shake my head, then it would land on my face again. When I looked out at Jack, standing there in the ditch, a fly crawled on his cheek. It stopped for a moment and rubbed its legs together but Jack still didn't swat it. He was just staring at something. Then, when I followed his gaze to the arm, I stopped shaking my head and just stared along with him. There were more flies, circling above it, crawling all over it.

I reach the end of the drainpipe. Looking out into the ditch, I half expect it to still be there, pale and bloated with the fingers half curled like dead flowers. But there is no arm, just ragwort and a coke can faded so it's no longer red but golden.

I can't turn around in the drain so I climb out and stand where Jack had stood. The mud is slicked beneath my school sandals. The rest of the walk home, I loop my string between my fingers in bows and knots. I count the movement it takes to make a cat's cradle. One two three four five . . .

Jack's in the lounge watching TV. He has physio every day after school and when Mum gets in she drops the groceries, huffs out her breath and calls, "Jack, come on. We're late." Then to me. "Help me get your brother in the car, please."

Jack does most of the work himself, dragging his legs into the front seat. I fold down his chair and push it into the boot. Then they're gone, zipping away in the new Honda, a snake of dust rising from the gravel driveway. I take out the string from the kitchen drawer and cut a piece as long as my forearm. I take a book from the shelf. The one with the rabbit standing on its hind legs on the cover. I wrap the string around it and tie it off with a double knot then I place it back on the shelf.

Dad gets home and I haven't peeled the potatoes so the first thing he does is pick up the remote and thrust it at the TV to turn it off.

"Potatoes, now," he says, all teeth and wide eyes.

"Okay."

Then he puts his work clothes in the wash and comes out

in a sweater and jeans. He goes to the fridge and grabs a Double Brown, when the can snaps open he closes his eyes and scrapes his palm up his forehead.

"Your mother out with Jack?"

"Yeah."

"You not giving her hell this afternoon?"

"Nope."

He clears his throat into his fist. "I've still got to go fix a trough in the paddock. Reckon you can cut those up and put them on the boil, after you've peeled 'em?"

I nod. He roughs my head and says "good man." Then he is out the door with his Double Brown and the motorbike starts up. Mum hates the four-wheeler, but Dad says we still need it. He says you can't blame the bike and I guess he's right. I used to ride it sometimes but last time I straddled the back of it, and started the engine Mum had rushed from the house. Her voice was stretched like old blue tack, Get down from there. She jerked me by my wrist. Then I heard a crack. I didn't realise what had happened at first, the left half of my face was hot and numb. Mum was just staring at her hand then she turned on her heels and paced back towards the house, leaving me standing there, crying.

I make some toast, picking the green bits off the bread and coating it with peanut butter. I know it's wrong to eat before dinner but Dad won't be back for a while.

I think of Jack sprinting across the lawn and Dad throwing the ball to him. Jack could catch it without breaking stride. Then he would fend off invisible tacklers, Dad saying, keep your knees up. He can't play rugby anymore, or leap fences, or pop possums from trees with the .22.

Dad is still out, and I've finished the potatoes. I sit in the wardrobe and close the door to trap the darkness in. I've got a seat made out of stacked boxes with my winter jacket over the top. I imagine cutting the string and wrapping it around the arm tight like a Christmas ham. I imagine wrapping Dad's cans of Double Brown, covering them all with string.

I imagine a world without birthdays or years. Instead we would count the days of our lives. We would celebrate milestones like your 3000th day alive. I might be 3000 today and no one would know and there's no cake, no candles, it's just another day. And I could remember days by their number, like the day dad found the dog-eared pornos Jack had stuck between my mattress and base. That could have been day 2732 or 2818 but I'll never know. I could remember the day of the arm 2921 and the day of Jack's accident 2925.

That night I hear them in the kitchen. Jack is in his room and it's one of those nights I can't stop my brain so I just lie there trying to be still and listening to the murmur of them arguing. Then when I get up and creep out slowly, the sounds become words.

"If we don't have the money we don't have the money, Tina," Dad says.

"Well what would you suggest we do?"

"Just make the most of a bad situation. I'd rather spend the money on something that makes him happy."

I just stand behind the door to the kitchen and a blade of light splits me in half, down my face, my torso to the ground.

"You could get some work, you know."

"Who will clean and look after him, then?"

"Who will watch the soaps, you mean?"

Mum breaks, just a little huff of air and when she speaks, I know she's crying.

"Don't touch me," she says.

"Alright, alright, I'm sorry."

I wish I had told them about the arm, it was Jack who said we better not. He said we would get in trouble for playing in the drain.

The next day I'm walking home alone, I'm at the spot where the tar beneath my sandals is soft and pliable. The spot where we had seen the police car leaning up the road's edge. I can almost see it now. There was yellow tape, bowed a little in the breeze. A man was sitting with his legs out of the open car door and a woman was pacing around the ditch with white gloves on.

When I got home, I put Rug Rats on to help me forget but some things don't leave my brain, some things follow my thoughts getting louder and louder, and even when I scream they're there. That's the arm, that's Jack's accident, that's the time Scott Reeves caught a wild cat and hung it by its back leg in a tree to shoot at with his slug gun, each shot a soft tap that rocked it, eventually it stopped mewling. Jack hadn't seemed too worried, lying there watching it. I never forgot.

I take the string out and the scissors. I cut lengths to go around the basketball, threading it, pulling it this way and that until the ball is covered. Then I start on the shell that Uncle Bill brought back from Fiji. I wrap it once, tie a knot then wrap it again and tie another knot. Then I start the book that says Pocket Editions: Science.

I remember the day they found out. Dad came home and he didn't take off his work clothes like usual, but went straight to the fridge and pulled out a Double Brown. Jack was on the four-wheeler, racing along in the paddock, maybe he knew they'd found out about the arm, maybe that's why he was out there so long. I was making my cat's cradles, doing them without looking, over and over, hovering near the sooty fireplace. Dad's shoulders slumped forward, his head nodded over the Double Brown.

He said, "Did you hear about the arm?"

Mum said, "What?"

"Apparently someone's found an arm, just off the road up near McGregor's."

"An arm?" Mum had said, her voice came over the knock-

knock-knock the knife makes when she cut the carrots. She turned back, her nose screwed up. "What sort of arm?"

"A human arm. Grim, I know. They don't know where it's come from, washed down after the storm."

Mum looked at Dad then jerked her head at me. "Oi," he said, turning back. "Go watch TV."

I didn't think about where the arm came from, just that I was glad I didn't have to tell them. They never found out that we were there, that we saw it. They didn't even talk about it again. I guess they didn't have time to think about it much after we had sat down for dinner and Dad looked up then said, "Hey, where's Jack?"

After the summer break everyone is still talking about the arm but I can't bring myself to tell the story of finding it with Jack. No one's really talking about Jack at all, except Cody, who's a year older, had said low and mean, your brother's a retard now. I just kept walking by like I didn't hear, squeezing the insides of my pockets in my fists. I don't think it will matter to me soon because Dad's saying we are going to go away. He's saying we are going on a holiday. He's saying we may even go to Disneyland. Just thinking about it now, it's like I'm already there.

'Days of Our Lives' was first published in **takahē 89** (April, 2017).

J.P grew up on a horse-racing farm in Rotorua with two brothers, a sister, two cats and two border collies. A first love for literary fiction quickly developed into a taste for sharp, fast paced story telling. Stories that surprised him, stories that tied a cold knot in the pit of his stomach. His work has been widely published in journals here and overseas, and he has won and been short-listed for a number of prizes.

J.P. has published three best selling novels, *Call Me Evie*, *In the Clearing*, and *Tell Me Lies*. His next novel *The Last Guests* will be released in 2021. J.P. currently lives in Australia.

the names in the garden

Tracey Slaughter

I do the flowers. I've always done them. They asked me not to this time, they took me aside and they told me, but I still had the key, so I let myself in. I lay them out on the bench like I've always done. I go by feel, I've never known the names. So I lay them all out. To look at which ones can take the weight, and which will have to drape. There are some that can stand for days, and some can only trail. Some are tough, but then the limp ones could be where the beauty is. But you work that into it. That all comes in to how you see it. They're out on the sink and you take a long look and you can see where the backbone is, and where there's just threads. Or whispers,

I don't know. Bits that catch the light, that's what I'm trying to get at. It just comes to me, when I take a slow look at them, spread that way. The centre stands out, the bloom that takes the eye right down into it, the place that needs to be the heart which all the rest weave round. There's always one you don't notice in the cutting, that rises out when you take them all in. Even if it takes me a while to find it, I stay calm and just keep watch. And then you see it lift itself out from the rest, and the others just nest in around it where they need to, or link at the base and spray.

So I'd had to let myself in. And the talk with the pastor had been hard, about how they didn't want me to go on doing it. And so I made a mess of it. When really I wanted to show them. I wanted to do something that would make them stop and hold their breath. And for that young couple, something they could join their hands by on the day and we could look up from the pews and it would be like the front wall poured with flowers and the whole church could feel white spilling all round from what I'd made. I thought I would. I had the key, and I told myself, I'll do what I always do, and I'll lay them in the good light out the back and if I watch them long enough they'll fall into shape. I thought I would see, glowing there right on the sink, the core of the thing. I could pick out the soul of it. But I hadn't been let in to the gardens. The people that usually let me come round and do the cutting had said no. The pastor had told me. He said people were uncomfortable. The families.

I said, *But nothing was proven.*

And he said, *But as things stand, it looks bad.* So I asked if I could just take the ones near the gates. I wouldn't even go in. They wouldn't even have to see me—though they always used to wave at me when I did the cutting, they used to send their little ones out to help me pick and to carry, and they used to chatter away. But the pastor said no, that a clean break was best now for everybody. The families entrusted him to make it clear to me. And then I said I would just kneel down by the fence, where there's even lovely heads that poke out through the bars and I could snip them off and no one would even know I'd been. And when he got short with me I said, *My husband never sets foot. He's never even in the same street. It's only me in the gardens.* I said, *Please. It's only ever me.*

But he made it clear I couldn't go in. Not even near. It was what they all wanted. It had been decided. All those gardens, where they used to let me in to take anything I needed. All those blooms and the green and the little girls dancing out to keep me company while I moved the fronds and leant down deep to cut low through the stems.

And so when I laid them out I couldn't see it: the one to give the centre, the shape. I did what I always do. But it wouldn't come to me. I took down the bowls and the traps and the oasis, and I stared at them too. It was very quiet, except for the long line of humming that comes off the new light. It makes that back room very bright and, true, it's a good light for doing the flowers in, but it does get up under the lids of your eyes, a white line of it that feels like grit. After a while, it seems to press right round the back of them, the buzz of it. So you blink and blink. And the bowls don't help, either. They have some beautiful vases, my church. So heavy. Like offerings. Some of them you have to pick up and hold like children, the colour of pearls. There's one I like that's got some finish on it, running down its sides like oil, only white, white oil with a kind of silver clearness that gives you the shivers. Or at least it does me. Like freezing silk to touch. But then it's a chore to pick up. It's a beauty, but a dead weight, and it slips. Or at least, I get full of the fear that it will and my heartbeat gets into my hands and makes them dizzy. And once it's packed out then I have to get help in to do the lifting onto the altar. With all the weight of the flowers wired in, it's too much for an old body like me. I don't have a chance of raising it up.

So I don't know what I was thinking, letting myself in, trying to change what they thought of me. It's just that I'd always done the flowers. So it didn't seem like it could be the end. I hadn't thought it through, but then I never need to think the flowers through. They just come to me, where they should be, and whether they should push up into crooked knots or they should hang down like a net, and whether they want to drift out and touch lightly as froth or they want to shoot and be twisted. They've always joined for me, in my eye, before I even started to touch them. And I thought for a moment that a flash did come, of how to work it, like the ripples of a star if you were too close to it, like its glory would make you weep but also had a sting to it. But then it went out. Just out, like the dark in its place in my head had always been there. A cold black I couldn't shift was just waiting in my head behind all the beautiful things I used to see. Then I found that I couldn't keep myself steady. There wasn't any calm left.

And I made a mess when I stopped looking and I started to handle them. Because I don't know the names in the garden where I've always gone, but I know them all by feel. And it was hard to find anything, when they said I couldn't come. I had no sense of where to go. I had to go creeping all over town, and it didn't seem like anything good was growing. Not where I could get to it, not without asking. And the way the pastor had made it sound to me, everyone felt the same, and I wouldn't be wanted even outside of the gardens, even strangers would know when they looked at me, they would have heard the stories. Only he said the news, not the stories.

As if it had turned into truth already. When it hadn't. I saw that news too. I stood by our letterbox on the day it came and opened the page and it was like the sun went out, and the words had shadows that rushed right through our front yard and I knew when I turned around they'd be all over our house and they'd be there too when I looked down our street. The thick ugly words they use in their headlines, moving down the street like weeds. I think I said that to the pastor, even. I said, *I knew those stories were spreading like weeds. But I didn't think they would get into the church.* But he said he had a duty, he said the feelings of the decent community would be with the poor little girl. So I walked around after that looking for blooms and I couldn't bring myself to ask, even when I saw what I needed, not if it meant I had to look at doors opening and decent people staring down into my face and thinking ugly things of me. So I wasn't left with much. And when I found something that gave me some hope it was down in the gully on the river-end of our street, where I've always shrunk from going. I've never had to go there because the gardens were open to me. But now, being shut out, it seemed like the only thing I could do was go down into that gulf. So I made myself cross over. And the fence into it had been broken. And the trees were thick and cramped me, and the smell soaked into my clothes. And the cold feel got deeper. And the dirt plugged up my shoes and they weren't even dry when I let myself into church later, so I walked it in with me, the smell of that swamp. It was steep down, so everything felt tipped on a slant. I wasn't dressed for it and I tore something I'd kept nice for years. And I had a hard time not slumping right into the muck. But I did find flowers there. I'd always known that I would. I'd just never looked.

So I let myself in. And I still had hope, that I'd see something shine up into my eyes when I looked at them. They hadn't looked in such a poor state on their bank. They'd looked hardy enough, quite stubby, and they had a rich leaf and a sprinkle of gold in the head. But I could see from the start when I let myself in, that something had happened to them. I don't know when. They were lovely, but you could see that the light had leaked out. There were breaks all through them, and juice came out the crushes in their stalks. The damage was done. It must have been moving them. I didn't notice. I wasn't ready to give up, though. And I thought I could anchor them, and make them prop each other up, I thought I could stake them so they didn't give way. So I started to wire them. But the wire seemed to mash right through the stems, and all I had were tangles of wet. I kept sweeping through them and trying to find one more I could brace. Then the next one turned to waste. And all I had made was a pile of shreds. And my hands were stained with the white sap that leached out of them.

I knew then that this was the end. It was that slimy milk that came off the plants. You couldn't scour it off. It stained. I just wanted all the foul things gone. I started to push the whole mob of flowers down the bin. They were useless. But I couldn't take the sickly feel of them sliding down my fingers. It showed up in the creases of my hands like it did on the stems, the glint of it sticking in the bruises. And then somehow I started thinking of the day when I married my husband and of how we'd been standing in a halo of stiff white flowers and it was lovely but then he couldn't get the ring to fit. And everyone was looking and he was annoyed and had to get hold of my wrist and push and push and I watched the skin of my finger lift up in red bands, and it stung and I bit down under my veil until it slid.

But then I came round. It wasn't clean out back of church, in the good light. The flowers had bled and bled. And I just wanted all the good things kept away from them. Their wet and their stink. And that's when it happened. Because I was in a rush. I wanted all the offerings back in their place again; the vessels, the vases with their skin like pearl. I wanted the bowls stowed away again, heavy and holy. I wanted to know that at least I'd kept sacred things safe. And the roar of the bowl blowing open seemed to pound through my ears when I never even felt the sides slip. Everything seemed to go backwards through my wet hands, and my eyes were

the names in the garden

a shatter of sharp white when I don't know if I ever really watched its body smashing open at my feet.

But if I did, I left the mess. I don't know how, I just left it. And I don't know how I got home, but once I got there I knew that he was gone. I did check. I walked through all the rooms, looking for a sign of what he'd left, and what he'd taken. And nothing had changed. He hadn't touched a single thing. But you could feel that he was gone. He'd just moved out, after all these years, and hadn't paid anything for all the time he'd stayed here, like a bad tenant leaving in the night.

So I went outside to the shed where I knew my husband would be. To tell him God was gone. But of course, he was gone as well. Although he had left me to clean up. And they made more headlines out of him too. Perhaps he thought he'd put a stop to that. He could kill the words off along with him. But the words go on and on. The black weeds, there's no end to them. They're like the things they've been bringing up out of that gully, terrible dark arrangements that don't have names. And now there's no place for me, I can't keep them back with white flowers.

I never went back to the church to clean up my mess. But then, neither did God.

Photo Credit: Joel Hinton

'the names in the garden' was published most recently in Tracey's short story collection **deleted scenes for lovers** (VUP, 2016).

Tracey Slaughter's latest collection of short fiction *Devil's Trumpet* was published in 2021 by Victoria University Press. She is the acclaimed author of *deleted scenes for lovers* (VUP, 2016), *Conventional Weapons* (VUP, 2019) and *The Longest Drink in Town* (Pania, 2015). Among other awards, in 2020 she won the Fish Short Story Prize and her novella *if there is no shelter* was published in the UK by Ad Hoc Fiction, as runner up in the Bath Novella-in-Flash Award. She teaches Creative Writing at the University of Waikato, where she edits the literary journals *Mayhem* and *Poetry New Zealand*.

Nineteen Seconds

Russell Boey

Clear.

Sometimes I have this nightmare that I can breathe underwater. I don't realise immediately. I hold my breath as the cold gnaws and I kick down. Below me his ankle circles in languid orbit, brushing on tangleweed. Deeper. Breath disappears with the last beams of light, but I don't stop; God knows I don't stop.

When I am certain that I will die, when I am sure that his sallow ankle will drift out of sight, I inhale a great gulp of water. It tastes of roast potatoes and carnival hot dogs. And I am still breathing.

I go deeper. I swallow the nauseating water and I keep

kicking, even though my legs ache under the pressure. When the sunlight is crushed, my eyes glow with the anglerfish phosphorescence my brother and I once saw on TV2, and I can see his ankle still spiralling, spiralling, sinking. By now the pressure has compressed my feet into flat paddles. If I look back, I can see where the bone has shattered, and if I don't focus on his ankle, the agony of each kick will make me pass out.

I try to imagine that I am a merman, growing a flimsy, fleshy tail. My brother used to like this show about mermaids. Maybe he found them pretty. He'd watch anything about the sea, any documentaries we could catch on the bulky TV which hung above his bed – The Silent World or Attenborough and Animals – so that if the day came when he metamorphosised out of his hated body, he would know all the dangers.

Once, beneath the dingy yellow light that flickered every nineteen seconds, we caught Creature from the Black Lagoon. Attenborough didn't narrate it. Horror was out of his field, but not ours.

This nightmare does not end. The ocean eats more of me, flattening me until I am no longer a merman but a great long eel, thrashing about in the wide cosmos, and still I cannot grab his ankle.

Clear.

Sometimes I have his dreams, like the one he came up with on the Waterfall Track thirty years ago. We'd driven up to Hanmer Springs on a family trip. We'd listened to Bon Jovi belt Living on a Prayer on the radio and he'd sung until he'd run out of breath.

He told me later, beneath the nineteen-second yellow light, that when we turned into those secret forests, he thought that he'd seen a dryad. He'd seen her flitting across the treetops, sometimes as a kingfisher, sometimes a fantail, sometimes a wrinkled face etched into a great bough. When he'd gone off the trail, he'd thought she was singing to him, in the birdcall and the distant trickle of water.

At the waterfall, with Mum still panting up behind us, he stared into the surface. I would grow used to his dreaming look in time, yellow light flooding the valleys of his eyes. But back then it was something special, and in that sacred place, the ghost of a dryad lingering, he seemed his own fantastical creature.

We knelt down by the place where the water fell, washed our hands in the pool. Together we scanned the surface, though I didn't know what I was looking for. When he saw me staring with such focus, he chuckled to himself in his mystic way.

'You're the best,' he said, and I did not reply, because there were no more words then than there ever were or would be.

When Mum caught up, we ate sandwiches by the rocks. After his third bite, I heard him cough.

Clear.

Sometimes I dream of the third of September in 1988, when I entered my brother's room for the first time in two months. I fluff the pillows and beat the dust off the seashells on his duvet. I cover my mouth when I cough.

I peel the glow-in-the-dark constellations off the walls. The glue leaves scars in the shape of Orion. They have no more light in them when they fall.

I leave the stars in a burial mound. I take Dune from his shelf and stow it into a cardboard box. I do not read the card I wrote to go with it two Christmases ago. It would have made me cry. Nor do I remove the get-well-soon cards from the shelf, collected over the course of three years. I pluck the vinyl figures of Batman and Robin from the windowsill and stuff them into the boxes, as if hiding all reminders will make them disappear completely.

In that dream, when I stack his clothes into the boxes and shuffle them to the side, the wardrobe opens to a fantasy, like in the book with the witch and a wonderful lie about coming back from the dead. He picks up the toys that lie scattered in the closet – the dog with one worn-out eye, the astronaut painted over with bright neon colours, the squid with its stupid smiling face – and he is smiling, and he is whole, not a carcass with a needle in his arm, wasting beneath the heat of a yellow light. It is five years ago again, and he is swinging a toy lightsabre in careless arcs around my face.

In that dream, I play with him until nightfall. I listen to him talk about the useless facts he picked up from the TV in the living room. I do not tell him that I need to study maths. I hum Darth Vader's theme and make the firecracker sounds when the blades clash. I cherish the sound of his breathless laughter as we dance around the room, luminous long after sunset.

In that dream, when the light is low and we are alone, lit by false skies, there is a stillness. I would wait there forever if I could, in that dark and fragile island.

'What are you thinking?' he asks.

I am thinking of a weak moment when, after Mum screamed at me for bringing him out to a carnival while he lay silent and paralysed beneath the yellow light, I hated him. But when I turn to confess, he is gone.

In that dream, I leave the closet behind. I close the door and let the cardboard spacesuit rot away in dust. I step up onto his bed and pull the duvet up over my head. I coil into a small and meaningless thing. Only then do I cry.

Clear.

Most often in my dreams I'm being chased by a dog. It runs me out of the hospital at the corner of Riccarton Avenue. I was there last in 1988, at 10:45pm. I take off past the coffee shop towards the Avon, but the roads are empty, and their signposts only read the years. Streetlamps guide me towards the river. The dog behind me pants, relentless sound of a running corpse, its eyes burning through the soft streetlights.

The sign which should read Antigua Street reads 1992. I hide on a plane to escape, but the dog's laboured pants still draw nearer. The runway lights flicker, and in that moment of darkness there is a shift.

1994. The dog stalks at the back of the nightclubs; it watches me each time I stumble on my words or trip on my own feet. The beat pounds every noise from my head except for the dog's growls. While I'm drinking my way through another conversation the dance lights flicker.

1996. Graduate. This time it's science, other times medicine, other times fine arts; it doesn't matter. I hurl my mortarboard backwards like a frisbee, but it doesn't distract the dog; nothing distracts the dog. Get a job. Sometimes it's at an office, sometimes at a bank, sometimes at McDonalds. Outside, the golden arches flicker.

2005. Come back home, back to the cemetery on

Avonhead. The dog's fur is black, to blend in with the mourners. We lay Mum into the ground and I don't cry. The grave dirt is hurled on, and some choir of birds or children or cruel angels play the dirge. Once the faceless black forms depart, I turn to the two headstones in front of me. I have forgotten to bring flowers.

Only then does the dog leap, knocking me between the graves of my brother and mother. Claws dig through my coat and draw blood, as his hands once did when he gripped my arm too hard during Nosferatu. The dog wears a hospital gown, and its face is the thin gaunt face of a boy, flecked with spit and blood. He digs his nails into me, drags them over my skin, but I cannot scream. 'Say something!' he demands, pathetic voice choked by phlegm and bile and blood. 'Say something!'

And I try, God knows I try, but there are no more words then than there ever were, and no more lights to flicker and save me, nothing but the dim glow of his fading dreaming eyes.

Clear.

This is what remains when I am not dreaming. White walls smudged with streaks of dirt. The head-in-hands position of mourning. The chair outside his room which has two loose screws and which groans when I rock, hands locked between my knees. Mum's hand on mine, two pairs of eyes on the flimsy door ahead. The peals of the clock above his room. 10:38. Three more minutes.

Three more minutes. Perhaps that is all I have. Perhaps I am in the same room as he was thirty years ago, beneath the same yellow light, jolted by the same metal pads, dreams and memories returned and stolen by the same shock of lightning.

'Come on,' Mum says. Her voice aches.

When I stop dreaming, I see him as he was, in the flimsy bed. I see his gaunt face lit by the crackle of the nineteen-second lightbulb. I see his eyes on the boxy TV above his head, still dreaming of all the magic he used to see, trying to squeeze infinities into the three years the doctors offered him. I cannot bring myself to look again. I shake my head.

Mum is too tired to glare at me. Her concern is spent elsewhere. 'You'll regret not saying goodbye.'

But there are no more words – no words sufficient in all the gaping skies and devouring seas. I shake my head again.

Stupid hopeless fool.

She goes in alone. She hides the view inside with her wracked frame. When she closes the door, I sit and rock on the squeaky chair and watch the clock toll towards 10:41. Outside I imagine the bottomless oceans that accept all that is, all those dead things trapped beneath, frozen in the dark.

Clear.

Then there is a room, and a clock at 10:40, and a squeaky chair, and nothing else. And maybe the ticking is not the clock but my own heart, high on lightning. The hospital peels away, the dirty white walls, the chair, and there is only me and this room, claustrophobic and dim and urgent.

The lightbulb keeps time. He lies in his gown with his dreaming eyes locked on the ceiling. Flicker. I sit down by his side. I do not look away from the ghostly face or lock my eyes on the TV's fantasies. His hand is still warm. Flicker. What does that give me? Twenty seconds? I have thought of goodbyes for thirty years. They are my fantasies. They are the dreams that I painted on the sanitised roof with my eyes, stars on the cold ceiling.

He would have killed for twenty seconds. Ten. Somehow, it will be enough.

'See you soon.'

Maybe those are all the words that ever were.

At the ending, when the doctor's gloves come off, when the shocks can no longer restore my dying heart – then all peels away, like septic skin, like a last cough in a cold room, like the final flicker of yellow.

Clear.

'Nineteen Seconds' won the **2020 Sunday Star-Times short story competition** in the under 25 category.

Russell is a physics student at the University of Auckland, focusing on astronomy. He has been writing since he was twelve, and his work has always been inspired by stars. When he isn't studying or writing, he enjoys board games and long walks.

Atul

Nithya Narayanan

Atul was waiting in the arrivals lounge. He was tall, lean and wiry, with a grey-speckled beard. A mole adorned his lower lip, and he was totally bald. Lauren surveyed him for physical similarities to herself. She found nothing.

'Lauren,' he said, smiling.

Should she hug him? Shake hands? How exactly did you greet the father you'd never seen before?

'I'll take that,' he said, reaching over to pick up Lauren's bag. The effort seemed to unbalance him, and for a moment he teetered. Lauren stuck her arm out.

'I'm fine,' he said.

'I can carry it,' said Lauren. 'Honestly.'

'I'm fine,' he repeated, but Lauren noticed his shallow panting as they made their way to the carpark.

***

His message had arrived two weeks ago. *Hello, Lauren, this is Atul Kapoor. I'm calling to invite you to Wellington. Perhaps you'd like to visit me this summer...*

'He's a selfish bastard,' her mother had said. 'It's a ploy.'

'A ploy for what?' Lauren had asked.

Later, she would look back and realize that she'd accepted Atul's invitation mainly out of loneliness. She'd grown sick of the banal pattern of her life—the nights spent in front of the television; the long, protracted silences. With the arrival of Atul's message, some part of Lauren had begun to entertain a hope that she might move in with him; that she might, at sixteen, finally feel part of a real family.

'He's a philanderer,' her mother had said, in parting. 'You wait and watch. He's probably got illegitimate children stuffed up his kitchen cupboards.'

***

In the car, Atul played Cyndi Lauper. He told Lauren that he lived in Miramar, on the peninsula. On the way there Lauren closed her eyes, relishing the sound of the sea.

'What's it like?' she asked him.

He glanced at her. 'What?'

'Living next to all this water.'

'A-ma-zing,' he said.

Inside Atul's flat, the walls were a seaweed green. The

place was small, the furniture all pressed together. The strobe lights in the living room were the only sign of extravagance. Atul spent most of the day upstairs, but in the evening he cooked for her: lamb biryani and microwaved poppadum. There was something about having a meal with another person—the intimacy of it—that Lauren loved. Her mother rarely cooked. Most of the time Lauren ate microwaved dinners alone. Her mother, who came home after eleven, would eat the leftovers while reading case briefs.

Atul was different. He was animated, attentive to everything Lauren said. When he laughed his whole body curved in on itself, his head dipping so low that it almost touched the plate.

'Why'd you shave off your hair?' asked Lauren.

He smiled at her. 'Hair is annoying.'

***

The next morning, Atul made her two burritos for breakfast.

'Eat quickly,' he said. 'I want to show you the art room.'

As Lauren ate, he swallowed two coloured pills from a bottle.

'What sort of stuff do you paint?' asked Lauren.

'I used to be really into surrealist stuff,' he said. 'At art school they called me the brown Magritte.'

Lauren had no idea who Magritte was.

'Quickly, quickly!' sang Atul, pointing to the food.

Lauren stuffed the remaining burrito into her mouth, startled by the urgency in his voice.

He led her up a short, cramped flight of stairs. By the time they reached the top he was panting again. This time the sound startled Lauren, unsettled her.

He said: 'Close your eyes.'

She did. Shutting her eyes reminded her of Christmases at her grandparents' home in Bucklands Beach. She remembered the somnolent purring of the cat, the early morning light filtering into the living room, the syrupy Christmas films that they'd watch together afterwards.

Her mother was never present in these memories. Her mother took on clients right through the holiday period, and if she wasn't working on Christmas day, she was usually asleep.

'Open your eyes,' said Atul softly.

Lauren did, and saw that they were standing in a room full of canvases. There were some paintings of the sea, of the winding road that they had travelled across to reach Atul's flat. Mostly there were just paintings of people. In one corner there was an oil painting of a girl. With a start, Lauren recognized her own blunt features.

'Is that me?' she asked in wonder.

Atul smiled. 'It's not finished yet,' he said.

***

Atul

That night, he asked if she'd ever done weed. She looked at him to see whether he was joking. His face was completely serious.

He went over to the kitchen cabinet, pulled upon a cupboard, and produced a plastic box of brownies.

'My stash,' he said, grinning. 'Care to join me?'

Nervousness pooled in Lauren's stomach and then, hot on the heels of that, a feeling of rebelliousness. She imagined her mother's shocked face. In the end, it was the deliciousness of that vision which impelled her to agree.

Atul led the way back to the art room. Dusk was falling, but he didn't turn on the lights. The two of them sat side by side on the floor. Lauren took a brownie and bit into it.

'I wonder what your mother would say about this,' said Atul, after a while. Lauren could hear the smile in his voice.

'She'd ask rhetorical questions,' said Lauren. 'Lauren Young, are you aware that you are breaching the Misuse of Drugs Act?'

Atul burst out laughing. 'Oh, Lorraine. Oh God, she was delightful. I think she was the smartest woman I ever slept with.'

The absurdity of the comment set Lauren off. Soon they were both in paroxysms, falling against one another in the darkness.

'But no, seriously,' said Atul, gasping for breath. 'A

Shortland Street lawyer. Your mother has done well for herself, hasn't she?'

'Sure,' said Lauren. 'So well that I never see her bloody face.'

The bitterness in her own voice surprised her. Wasn't it because of her mother that she was able to live the life that she did? There were plenty of fatherless kids at Lauren's high school, and she'd seen enough of them to picture the route her own life might have taken. Still, she resented her mother; resented the many nights, growing up, that she'd spent at her grandparents' home.

'I'm sorry,' said Atul. 'I've said something I shouldn't have.'

Lauren didn't know if it was the cannabis, but she felt, suddenly, a strange kinship with Atul. She felt a giddy delight. It did not matter that she did not know who Magritte was. It did not matter that she did not have Atul's lovely dark skin, his black hair.

'Can I live here with you?' she asked abruptly. She had not planned to ask him so soon, but the words seemed to burst from her, almost against her will.

There was a long pause. Then Atul turned to look at her, his face inscrutable.

'Lauren,' he said, 'there's something you should know.'

He told her that he had lung cancer. He told her that he'd

refused treatment. He told her all of this in a soft, matter-of-fact voice, as if he was announcing the next day's lunch menu.

Lauren stared at the wall. She felt numbness and then, overwhelmingly, anger. He had invited her into his life only to announce its end. The neatness of the operation—the finality of it—incensed her.

'How long?' she asked, finally.

Atul shrugged. 'I don't know. It could be three months, a year.'

She got to her feet.

'Wait,' he said. He went over to the far wall and picked up the painting of Lauren. 'I finished it last night. I want you to have it.'

Lauren hefted the canvas. Yesterday it had looked small, deceptively slight. It was only now, when she held it, that she realized how heavy it really was.

'Atul' is previously unpublished.

Nithya Narayanan is pursuing a BA/LLB (Hons) at the University of Auckland, where she is also Co-Editor-in-Chief for *Interesting* journal. She has completed two creative writing courses with distinction at the New Zealand Writers' College. Her poetry and essays have previously appeared in *Starling, Mayhem, Minarets, NZ Poetry Shelf* and *Best New Zealand Poems 2019*. She was one of the Epigraph Project's featured writers in 2020.

Gutting
Ting. J. Yiu

It unsettles Kim how she's become the face of the tragedy. The dog lady who discovered the whale stranding. The reporter smiles a mouth only smile and when she doesn't respond he repeats himself.

"How did you find the whales, Ms Liu?"

Rutherford's tail thumps against Kim's legs. He pulls against his leash, nuzzling the reporter who looks out of place against the West Coast sand. Rutherford barks. Kim wishes she'd kept him home.

"Ms Liu?"

"My name is Kimberley. Kim." She looks away from the camera, staring at the grey-green horizon, focusing on anything but the hundreds of too-still bodies scattered over the volcanic sand.

***

She had watched uneasily as strangers poured into their village after the discovery. The Project Jonah rescue people arrived first, lugging safety equipment, flotation devices and high-visibility vests. Then a helicopter, the whip of its propeller blades flattening a circle of tussock as a scientific team tumbled out onto the beach; a marine biologist: a conservation ranger and two PhD students from Otago. By Saturday, the place had spilt over with outsiders. Cars and utes settled on the grassed embankment like a mob of sandflies. Surfers in the bullet grey water trying to corral endless pods of incoming whales back to sea. Local school kids and teachers scooping streams of water over the animals, trying to keep them hydrated.

"I won't be staying," Kim had said when a boy asked if she wanted to help.

"Why?" he stopped petting Rutherford's head, "they need us."

There were at least three hundred whales, more beaching by the hour, and these strangers had stayed awake all night to help. She knew with a terrible certainty that they couldn't save them all. Some whales were near the end, their breathing ragged, laboured, and many of the mothers were baying, surrounded by their calves, already dead.

"I'm sorry" was all she had said to the boy, as she led Rutherford away.

HUNGER
Did I already know then,
the year they flooded Beijing
on that submerged swampy summer,
that it would for nothing?
We believed,
thought saviours of ourselves,
of their hunger sharpened eyes,
of people, swarming streets like fireflies.
Allowed myself to be swept,
by fleshy solid newness.
Even when they said they'd clear
the gathering
by whatever means.
Meaty belief coloured the air,
even our elders,
stockpiling rakes and pickaxes,
gathering rocks, mixing petrol bombs.
Even Mr Hua, who butchered entire cows
with a few strokes of a cleaver,
who downed sorghum wine like water
and stole money from customers.
Even the butcher said,
they can try
but they'll have to come after us first.

"If you could just run us through how you found them," the reporter asks, impatience breaching his voice.

She imagines the 6 o'clock news, her face broadcast into millions of Kiwi homes. They will see a middle-aged Chinese woman, eyes placid, even against this tragedy. She knows how they will think, "You just witnessed a whale stranding, where is your compassion?" The word that appears in their minds would be—as if out of nowhere, agreed collectively about her kind—emotionless.

She stares into the camera, seeing her warped face projected back. The sameness spooks her—the cameras, the questions, the journalists. An urgency to record a cargo of limp bodies and carnage.

Rutherford barks and she is snapped back to the present. The West Coast. The beach. The whales. She exhales. Tells herself, I am in New Zealand, the ground here is solid. My name is Kim, and this is my home.

"Kim?" a shard of uncertainty pries itself through the reporter's camera-ready veneer.

Rutherford becomes cagey, bouncing from paw to paw. She lays a hand on his head. It must be the dying whales, maybe he can smell something on the animals that she can't. Or maybe, he can smell something on her.

Everything dies, she thinks, sinking her hand into his salt-crusted, still-damp pelt. Everything.

***

Rutherford found Kim eight years ago. He'd appeared in her garden one day after heavy rain, no collar, thin. She'd watched from behind the screen, eyeing the grey creature slumped under her cabbage tree. It scared her, his tired eyes, trained on the house. She'd quietly backed indoors, not even removing her shoes, and double bolted her door.

She thought she'd heard him circling the property, like a night prowler. She'd kept her lights on until dawn, but in the morning, he was still there watching. She sprayed him with water, then threw stones at him, but they all landed without him flinching, his sad grey eyes still watching.

"What do you want from me?" she had yelled, her voice losing out to the omnipresent ocean roar crashing to shore.

The people who had sold her the house had not owned a hunting dog. Neither did anyone in the village. He was there the next day, and then the next. And he was there every day after that, late into the summer of 1992, until Kim forgot that he hadn't always been a part of her life and a part of this land.

She didn't let him into the house at first, only leaving out a bowl of water and some bones from the cattle farmers. In her childhood—at least how she chose to remember it—animals had never been friends. But slowly, imperceptibly, she grew used to, and even needed, his company.

Every morning, Rutherford would have the red leash in

his mouth, waiting by the side of her bed, nudging his warm nose into her face. By dawn, both of them would be trekking, slowly up the coastal path, for their bushwalk.

She named him after Ernest Rutherford, the New Zealander who had split the atom. When people remarked that it was an interesting name for a dog, she lied, saying it was a tribute to her adoptive home. She didn't say that her father had also been a physicist, who instead of fairy tales, had told her stories of scientists who pushed for truth and certainty and knowledge. As if names could actually change anything, she thinks now. Kim? Rutherford? Ridiculous shields to hide the truth of things.

***

"Where did you first see the whales, Kim?" the reporter shifts his right foot, leaving a crescent trail in the sand.

"At the lighthouse."

"The lighthouse?" his eyebrows raise, "isn't that quite far away?"

Kim doesn't like his tone. It feels all of a sudden like an interrogation with the camera trained onto her face. Kim points to the cliffs rising above the beach, the white lighthouse perched on top. The camera follows her gaze. "If you're accusing me of not reporting this earlier—"

"That's not what I meant."

"What are you saying then? I called as soon as I could."

"With mass standings, time is crucial. The sooner the authorities are alerted the better their chances of survival."

There it is again, his tone clipped and brusque as if she were a child. Of course, she knows about timing. She has medical training. Had medical training. After she moved here, she got as far away from wounds and pain and death as she could.

"They looked like driftwood from up there," Kim said.

"Driftwood?"

"Is this your first time on the West Coast, sir?" she looks him square in the eyes.

"No." He pauses, then adds "Ma'am."

Kim wants to spit into his face. Show him how the seas here are brutally rough. How storms rip entire trees and shipwrecks from the bottom of the Tasman, tossing them on the black sand like skeletons of the deep. Didn't he understand that this place didn't play games?

She draws Rutherford closer, steadying his head, stopping him from jumping up again. "I couldn't see from the lighthouse. I had to get down first before calling the coastguard. Ok?"

The West Coast is populated with descendants of mining families and nomadic Kai Tahu tribes. They lean against mine shafts and hand-hewn cabins, waiting for the sky to darken. Counting the rain beating into them sideways, knowing that the bush and moisture have been here longer than eight centuries of human settlement. Their faces say, I know the harvesting of river pounamu, giant slabs of black-green rock pulled barefoot with flax rope. They know the wrestling with ash grey tunnels to haul coal, unwilling, from the depths. The clawing of tea-coloured earth when walls collapse, darkness blanking the single point of exit. Roughness lingers in their slow drawl and even slower welcome of outsiders. It was the kind of isolation Kim had been looking for when she moved here. Anonymity. Remoteness. The possibility of disappearance.

She had taken on lighthouse duty because she thought that it would let her fit in. She wasn't about to invite people over for company. A monthly check was all that was needed but she had started doing the walks every week. Then daily, as if walking could be an act of cleansing. Or exorcism.

An hour up the bush track the landscape suddenly burst open, revealing the headland. Toetoe and bent-over kanuka fanned out towards where the lighthouse rose, like a white chess piece balanced on the cliff. Kim had to walk towards it until the horizon levelled out again and the stretch of black lava sand became visible, grey surf pounding in endless bands.

Sometimes Kim would sit with her binoculars, scanning the horizon. She watched black-billed gulls catch the wind, and lingered over bleached driftwood that had been flung ashore like secrets oxidising in the air. Even when there were no birds and the sea was flat, she would sit there, still, for hours, studying the expanse of remote emptiness that felt clean and unmarked.

WALKING

We walked Beijing like a game.
Ba asked if I could see his window
at the physics department.
In now extinct hutong alleys
we found tanghulu hawkers
guarding sticks of too-red fruit,
imitated the knife sharpener
with his operatic wail and grindstone.
Ba told me not to be rude
so I begged for jianbing
liang mao a piece that burned my tongue.
Tired and petulant, Ba hoisted me on his shoulders
while I gaped at street dentists
pulling teeth on the sidewalk
making theatre of bloodied gums and tongues.

I walk in New Zealand too
counting raw blisters and shin splints.

The game is finding the edge of the globe
where I recognise nothing
but give new names for old things
masticating unfamiliar sounds
in my ah-yee mouth.
In the South Pacific, anything can disappear
off the lip of the horizon
space is how I am unaccounted for,
a stranger, blameless and unmarked.
I have edged my toes over the cliff-ledge
lifted ankles, hamstrings taut,
watched rocks tumble downwards
to smash against ocean and salt spray
imagined the intake of breath
suspended in between falling
conjuring an Olympic diver's grace
swanning elegantly,
arms out, nose down
my body of veins and viscera slicing through air
where at the ends of the world
there is nowhere left to walk but sea.

It was foggy the day Kim discovered them. The shiny black bodies of the whales had been indistinct lumps against the dark sand. Identical oil-slick heads kerning into torpedo-shaped smoothness, foam spilling off their bodies. There were so many, it looked like an infestation, except they didn't move.

She sat at the lighthouse and waited, even after it began to drizzle, then pour. The deluge would leave nothing untouched. She unleashed Rutherford and turned, reluctantly, inland.

She started to sprint, roused by an urgent vision of carcasses and bodies in the tide. Ahead of her, Rutherford tore through the bush. Together they thundered through salt scrub, leaping over tree roots, Kim nearly turning an ankle on a stone. They veered right, banking into the stand of golden tussock that buffered the ocean from land. When they broke through onto the sinking sand, she could hear them.

They were not carcasses, they were alive. Calling to each other over the droning waves, thrashing dorsal fins slapping uselessly against the sea. Shallow surf broke over their backs making them gleam like polished onyx. They were the darkest things she had ever seen, as if they were black holes that could absorb all light. She didn't want to go near them, afraid to see her reflection in their skin. She watched Rutherford charge into the knot of whales. He sniffed one, then sprang back, as if hit.

"Come back!" Kim called.

He lifted his snout and ran, so fast it looked like he was

levitating. Flecks of slate-coloured sand flicked behind him as he bolted away from her. She hollered again, but her voice was stolen by the ocean's roar. She could still make him out—grey fur slicked smooth by rain—as he faded into the monochrome landscape. She did not want to go near them, but she forced herself onto the beach, feeling the hundreds of whales watching her with dying eyes.

When she finally found him at the farthest end of the beach, Rutherford was panting in front of a large mound of whales. They formed a solid mass behind him, a thick wall of drowning mammals, eyes reflective like dark marbles.

Kim avoided their gaze. "Guo lai," she said quietly, focusing only on Rutherford.

She held out dog biscuits. Nothing. She tossed one at him. It hit his nose and bounced onto the wet sand, untouched.

Row-ruff. Rutherford circled the whales, pawing the beach. He nosed the closest one, sat down, then barked again. Kim suppressed an unfamiliar rage, stopping herself from lunging over to clamp his jaw shut. The ease of their relationship betrayed—quite abruptly—by this strange urgency.

She ignored the pulsing mass of bodies, their iodine smell, their heaving breath. She kept Rutherford in her vision and in one motion, snapped the leash onto his collar.

"We have to go home!"

He dug into the sand. She yanked at the leash, unintentionally jerking his neck. Her frenzied terror came as a surprise. Rutherford made his body heavy and started whining, as if in chorus with the dying whales.

DIGGING IN
It was the summer of
hundreds of long-haired boys
with slim waists and slogans,
girls with big hair in polyester prints
with their placards and proclamations
chanting and starving in unison.
The place became a field hospital
my job to check saline drips attached
to young things lying inert on cots,
side by side, who called to each other,
with lips dried, desiccating in the summer sun.
I could have been them
stubborn young children,
but I shone nurses' torches into eyes
that glowed like marbles,
scanning for consciousness, hydration, sanity.
Stayed past my shift,
changed into plain clothes
to sit under makeshift tents,

listening to young people
with strength to sing after hungry weeks
refusing to leave
as the night drowned on.

—-

Kim forced herself to leave Rutherford on the beach. She had to make calls. It was a relief to get away from those staring animals with their marble eyes. She hugged Rutherford, scooped all the dog biscuits from her pockets and piled them beside him. And then she ran to escape the oil-slick bodies. She imagined the rain pelting Rutherford until he lost his fur, until he grew smaller and smaller as the mass of whales grew larger, each wave bringing in another mound of bodies until finally, he dissolved completely.

Kim made it home in under 20 minutes, crashed into the kitchen, grappled with the phonebook, leaving damp prints on the pages. She was shaking as she jabbed the numbers. Six rings until someone picked up.

"Wei?!.... I meanImeanImean Hello? Coastguard?"

"This the coastguard. Do you need assistance?"

"There are hundreds. So many. All over the beach dying. Hundreds. Please. Please."

"Ma'am? What do you need assistance with?"

"Whaleswhalesatthebeach!!!"

"Ma'am, slow down."

"Hundreds of whales stranded. At the beach. Please."

"I understand. I'm dispatching a boat now. They'll meet you there in thirty minutes."

She stripped out of her soaked clothes, changed into a heavy raincoat, canvas pants, gumboots. Grabbed three bath towels, the half-empty sack of dog biscuits, and crammed herself into her car, flooring it through the rain.

Only when she was parked at the beach did her vision begin to spin. Kim gripped the steering wheel, gulping air in shallow mouthfuls.

DEJA VU

The skies blistered and burned
heart thrumming too hard
legs and lungs searing as if fried
tearing away from the city's square,
running an impossible distance
until the hospital loomed
like a face, a mouth, waiting for a meal of bodies.
I ran as if they were chasing me.
Armoured creatures, beast with long noses
barrelling into children
a thousand-headed machine, made
of faceless country boys
vomiting metal into soft bellies and young heads.

—-

When the scientists arrive on Friday evening, the light is nearly gone. They join the coast guards and the Project Jonah rescue team who are working on a cluster of whales; wrapping towels over the bodies and digging moats around them. Kim watches them fill shallow trenches with seawater which they scoop over the animals, again and again, to hydrate their skin and stop them from desiccating. She turns away, blocking out the whales and the sea.

When they are done, she beckons the scientific team over. Wordlessly, she heaves Rutherford—fur still damp, wrapped in towels—into her arms, and trudges to her waiting car. For some reason, the group understands to not offer help, even as Kim's short frame is engulfed by the dog. Rutherford seems to weigh nothing, as if the rain and ocean have devoured him from the outside. The scientists follow the short Chinese woman who drives them to her home in silence. The enormous grey dog sits, curled in the front seat.

Kim shows them the toilet, the kitchen and the living room where makeshift beds have been made with spare mattresses. "I'll be in the granny flat if you need me."

The marine biologist, James, touches her arm before she leaves, "Thank you. We know it's short notice."

"It's fine." She studies his face, he looks to be the same age as her, but there is something in his eyes that reminds Kim of her father. She walks into the garden and hoists

Rutherford into her arms. Her knees crack as she bears his weight, treading barefoot over the rain-fed grass.

***

Kim wakes around four am. Where am I? Rutherford. Where is he? Oh. Granny flat. She slumps back into bed. Rutherford is sleeping by the door. She lies back down, watching his flanks rising with each breath.

She can still see them, heaving whales superimposed against the ceiling, side by side. She closes her eyes and they are still there, the gleam of their skin vivid, glowing.

"I will not walk to the lighthouse today," she decides.

Unable to sleep, she crosses the garden and slips into the house without a sound. She makes tea and takes it to the steps of her porch. A half-moon is surrounded by the last smattering of stars. The roar of the ocean travels over the range, even louder now that everything is asleep.

She tries to warm her chilled hands around the mug. She'd slept in all her clothes, yet it felt as if part of the sea rain had followed her home. The sliding door opens.

"Can I join you?" James mouths.

Kim nods, "There's tea in the kitchen."

They sit wordlessly in the dark. He drinks from the mug with the garish photograph of Hong Kong's skyline. The one she never uses. The one she bought when she left China and washed up in Hong Kong. It had been a talisman of sorts.

Now, it just seems naive. She drains her mug. "Why do they do that?" she asks, "why do they die together like that?"

"We have a few ideas," James rubs his face, "but it's still one of the mysteries of the sea. We don't know enough about their lives to make conclusive theories."

She sets her mug down, "What do you know?"

"Well, pilot whales are matrilineal. They live in pods of twenty to a hundred individuals, sometimes more. They navigate by echolocation—bouncing sound-waves through water to build a 3-D picture." James lifts the mug, staring at the image. "Extreme weather and unusual ocean topography confuse them. They swim to land instead of away from it,"

Kim watches him drag a thumbnail over the skyline as if trying to scratch the image off.

"Underwater radar messes—"

"Please don't do that," Kim says.

"Huh—?"

"You're scratching my mug."

"Oh. Sorry." Genuine surprise in James' voice, "I didn't realise."

"It's okay," she watches him set it down, but doesn't take her eyes off it. "You were saying?"

"Radar, offshore drilling, it ruins their navigation system. Sound travels kilometres underwater, magnified by thousands of decibels. Imagine having your ear right next to an airplane at takeoff. That's how loud it is for the whales. The ocean is not a silent place, it's deafening for everything that lives there."

How ironic, Kim thinks, that animals called pilot whales could lose their navigation and end up stranded like refugees in an alien land.

"How is it possible that they all lose their direction like that? There are hundreds of them." She studies his face, creases that seemed to dance on his forehead exactly like her father's did when he worked. "They don't or can't abandon their family pod. It's encoded, instinctual if you will, as if they are magnetically bonded to each other."

"It's mass suicide—" she whispered.

"Yes. Some call it that."

***

After breakfast, Kim drops the scientists back at the beach. She doesn't get out, but drives straight home and spends the day pretending to garden. Late afternoon, she forces herself into the house for a change of clothes. There are folders on her kitchen table. Duffel bags in the living room. Strangers' clothes hanging on the back of her chair. She's an intruder in her own home. She washes out the mug with the Hong Kong skyline and stows it at the very back of the highest shelf in her kitchen cupboard, rim down.

It is when she arrives at the beach to pick up James and his team that the reporter finds her.

"You see the whales for the first time. It's so difficult, so tragic. How did you feel?" he thrusts the microphone at her.

She can see the headlines. Disgruntled Local Disapproves of Whale Rescue. Rutherford has started again, pawing at the ground. The crowd seems to make him nervous. People digging moats, covering the whales with blankets soaked in water, carrying all sorts of containers—toy buckets, tin pails, chilly bins—dipping them into the sea, dragging them back to the mass of inert bodies, pouring water over them, most of it trickling back into the grey sand.

The air feels thin and shallow as if too many outsiders are breathing her air. The busload of teenagers now scooping water with jerky limbed loudness. The surfers past the breakers, scanning for whales trying to rejoin their pod. Outside families making an outing of it, their toddlers building obnoxious sandcastles beside hulking dying beasts.

The Project Jonah team are hoisting whales to the tide-mark. They sandwich them between inflated bolsters and swim two-to-a-whale, steering them away from the shore and away from their dead. They do this over and over again, for hours, hoping they will leave the dead to go back to sea.

A few swim away—if only momentarily—but the magnetic bond is too strong to be broken. They return, circling back, wave after wave, each time stranding themselves with purpose.

Fatigue sets in, people pause, drenched. Hands rest, nervous against foreheads. Some stare in defeat at the endless, incoming tide of mammals. Some cry. Others hug the whales, stroking them cheek-to-cheek, murmuring to them as if they are dying relatives. The marble-eyed giants blink but they are unmovable and determined.

MAGNETIC BONDS
I didn't ask for their names,
and I never told them mine.
I remember one young man
I wanted him to eat some congee,
tried to ease a spoonful into his mouth
porcelain knocked against teeth that refused to open,
he accepted only water.
he flashed a limp peace sign with his right hand
his smile stretched his cracked flaking lips.
They had been doing this for weeks.

How willing they were
stranding themselves in their city,
their 心肝,
loving it like their heart and liver,

in this hot, dirty place, of flying rubbish and canvas tents,
they were all the same,
from bed to bed, magnetically bonded
refusing to be saved,
banking together—all at once—like a family to shore.

By the end of the third day, those that have deceased begin to fill the air with their salt rot, attracting blowflies. A putrid sweetness clings despite the relentless pound of the Tasman on this lip of land that Kim calls her second home.

There are too many to transport so a bonfire is built near the cliffs where the flames can be contained. A construction company from Westport loans earth diggers with rolling caterpillar tracks. Their yellow machine bodies inch down the sand dunes, crane necks lift, themselves like creatures, moving inert bodies—carcasses limp, hanging—in grotesque procession, away from the sea.

She watches James supervising his students who carry a small whale on a stretcher. They disappear inside a white tent. He sees Kim and waves. She pretends not to see, turning instead to the jagged rock ledges below the lighthouse. She sees him jogging over and contemplates running back to the car. In that time, he has crunched over the tussock and is standing beside her.

"We're nearly done, Kim. Just a little bit left before we

pack it in. We can catch a ride with the Landes if you don't want to wait."

"No. It's fine."

CLEARING
Bodies
shunted to the side, under piles of wrecked bikes.
Torn shirts. Single shoes. Crushed spectacles.
A rumble of caterpillar tracks bearing down
towards the magnetic centre.
Air contagious. Sharp with panic.
Clothes red, gashed foreheads, hands to faces.
Stretchers made with benches, blankets, three-wheeled
flatbed trikes,
pulling through a pall of smoke and gas,
shots fired at anything that moved.

At four am, the hospital received its first meal
they had run here, barefoot
staunching legs, chests, heads,
thinking they could save limp bodies
that were already dead on arrival
A young woman clawed at me.
leaving streaks up my arms.
Not enough beds, we dragged mattresses from storage,

Turned hallways into makeshift wards.
Rising panic.
flee. Flee. FLEE.
More, pouring in like gluttony,
air thick with iron.

Five thirty am,
foreign camera crew washed in with the tide.
We dragged them through the mouth doors.
Film everything. Film it all, we pleaded.
Did they understand?
We waved x-rays in their faces,
Pointed at shrapnel
lodged
in faceless ribcages, organs, torsos.

From fifteen floors up,
We witnessed flares
ignite in orange flashes.
And smoke columns
gashing the sky open.

"Before we leave, let me show you something," James says.

"I don't—"

"Come," he says, leading Kim to the whales.

It's the first time she's looked directly at them. Some are clearly dead, overturned so that their rows of tiny milk teeth flash upwards, mouths open in tiny upside-down crescents. Project Jonah people cluster around a trio. The one in the middle is a calf, wrapped in wet towels like a second skin. When they get closer, she can hear it. A high-pitched squeaking that changes in tone, trying to communicate with its family, dead beside it.

Kim reaches out to its smooth skin, firm and resistant. She finds herself scooping water around the moated creature, adjusting damp towels. Light slips away behind the cliffs. She sees a long march of bodies spread out as far as the beach spans. It is endless and numerous and she thinks of the bonds that drove three hundred of these creatures onto their shore.

Is she in New Zealand where the whale blubber burns in a blistering heap, fat crackling orange in the air? Or is she back there, where rumours flew of bodies being bulldozed. Unwilling thoughts of magnetic bonds – the multiples ones she has broken – overcome her. In a flash, she gets up, "I'll wait for you in the car."

***

That night, in the cover of dark, Kim packs her hunting rifle, ammunition, a tent, food into her car. Rutherford settles in the front seat. She drives south, away from the beach, inland. She knows that she can no longer stay. She made the decision after James left her granny flat. She had held his dry hands that smelled like the outdoors tinged with the fainter, meatier scent of whales and blubber.

Up close, he hadn't looked anything like her father after all. She was unsure if she was disappointed or relieved. It had been a long time since she'd undressed a man's body. It had been a long time since she'd thought of her father. The proximity of those thoughts unsettled her.

It was the way she could smell the whale musk lingering on his skin. It was the look of floodlights lighting up the beach like a crime scene. It was how the diggers lifted the bodies dusted in the fine sand like icing sugar.

Kim drives, hard, so the wind stings her eyes. She opens the window, inhales the scent of trees and soil. She lets the wind blow away the salt. Absolve her from the mass stranding, the knots of people, the questions. She doesn't care that the team will wake up to find her gone. At least she left her keys. At least she wrote a note this time.

After an hour, she drives her car off-road into a gulley. She covers the hood and bonnet with branches and leaves. She unscrews the number plates, tucks them into her backpack and walks into the bush. At nightfall, she makes camp and builds a fire, staring into its embers until sleep overcomes her. After a day, she guesses that the reporters and crowds have left. Nothing left to save but a pile of charred bodies. She doesn't want to return. Not yet. On the third day, she nears the end of her rations. She will have to hunt the rest with Rutherford.

***

Hunting had come surprisingly easy to her, just like sloughing off China and slipping into a New Zealand skin had been easy. She had picked Kim. The Cantonese in Hong Kong told her it sounded like gold—golden name, golden future. That childish sentiment turns her stomach now.

Back then, Kim had stayed away from people and big cities. She took jobs where she could be alone. Lost amongst Marlborough orchards, she picked fruit for eight dollars an hour. The televisions of the campgrounds she stayed at always seemed to play hunting shows on repeat. Men hauling wild boar, deer, and chamois with their hands. Survivors. Self-sufficient. Uncomplicated.

She had heard that they sometimes gave basic gun training to conservation volunteers. She remembers the ranger, in his thick backcountry accent, saying that rabbits, possums, and cats were responsible for decimating New Zealand's native birds. This is how she would help this country, she thought then, ridding the islands of unwanted pests. She joined culling missions, sometimes even getting helicoptered in, to do battle against the encroachment of the foreign. Naive, she now calls it.

It began with something called spotlighting, sounding like an innocuous campground game played with torches and firelight. Really, it was four-wheeling the backlands with lights mounted on overhead racks, flooding the night with deceptively warm beams as if they were holding a midwinter party and would drink beer or dance late into the evening.

Except they were like a troop, gun-slinging with a kill list. The spotlights illuminated warm-blooded, rapid-hearted things scurrying the scrubland after dark. They shot at them, standing from the backs of trucks. In truth, she had wanted to know what guns and killing felt like. What the taking of a life meant. Is that what had happened then? Soldiers—country kids really—standing in rank, shooting at other unarmed kids?

But cats and rabbits are not people, Kim.

***

Now, she must catch one of those furred creatures for food. Rutherford runs ahead, sometimes looking back, burrowing at ponga stubs, trying to sniff them out. They watch soft-nosed rabbits picking up the scent of human and dog.

Kim aims. On her out breath, she shoots. Each time, Rutherford disappears into the undergrowth and returns with them, limp in his mouth. He never pierces their small bodies with his teeth, never tosses or tears at them. He lays them at her feet, whole.

Kim makes small cuts into the hind legs and in one rip the entire pelt slips off. A white membrane separates the connective tissue. She turns it on its spine and splits it upwards in the middle with a small flick. She cracks the ribcage to reveal the innards. The heart is the size of a walnut. Ribbons of nude intestines fill her palm. A liver purple and warm. Rutherford eats them from her hands.

PREMONITIONS
On Sundays Ba cooked chicken,
choosing jewel-coloured birds from the weekend market,
brought them home, live and feathered
with amber eyes and emerald tails.
I chased them—buk-bukking—from room to room.
Ba taught me to gut them over our dirt floor,
red blood dripping into brown earth.
Ba the craftsman, only in reverse,
pulling apart instead of putting together,
naming every organ.
I understood then, that Ba knew everything.
He sliced lobed lungs,
oblongs laced in a filigree of blue veins.
Excavated livers, gizzards, the heart

with confidence.
Used a spoon to scrape out threads of viscera,
unearthed yellow ovaries,
small marbles
twin suns glowing in the ribcage.
Still-warm, Ba dropped them into my seven-year-old palms
Later, I recognised my own twin suns
a rotating galaxy of a million eggs
that went entirely unused.

The next morning, Rutherford is missing. Kim calls into the bush but only insects and wind replies. The five rabbits she'd strung up between the trees are missing, the cord ripped. They were just high enough for Rutherford to reach. If he jumped, he could have torn the rabbits down. Kim finds gnawed bones on the ground.

She circles for hours, yelling her throat raw. She feels as if she's back at the beach when he ran away, thundering desperately towards the whales. She remembers hitting him in the snout when he refused to leave them. How she had coiled the leash around his legs so that he would stop thrashing, rolling his great grey body in towels and heaving him to her chest. She remembers the stones she threw at him on the first day. She remembers jerking his leash with outsiders watching.

Kim waits, not daring to leave camp unless Rutherford returns to find her gone. She rekindles the embers and makes her last packet of instant tomato soup as night falls.

***

Two days pass. Kim is running out of water. She has run out of food. She will need something bigger than rabbits. Wild boar. Or a deer. But she has only one round of bullets left. She heads downhill to find water. She hopes she can find her next meal. She hopes to find Rutherford more.

She lurches in circles through trees that look the same. Her knees crack and she feels old. She will not cry. This is her home. She will find her way out. She will find Rutherford.

Finally, there is a stream. She sups like an animal, plunging her whole face into the rush. She drinks until her stomach is bloated and her shirt darkened from spilt water. She feels ready. Ready to take herself a deer.

She imagines the hunt over and over again. She will melt into the bush, become invisible, rooted like the tendrils of ferns that will sprout from her head and bush frogs that will nestle in the crevices of her thighs. She will be so still that the deer will not smell her.

It happens quicker than she had imagined. A young doe

stepping into the clearing. A whoosh of the bullet and it is floored, thudding into the undergrowth just like that.

She must bring the body back herself. She lies on her back for hours, the gun beside her, staring through the tangled foliage which begins to swim and sway. She watches the sun pass overhead until it is late afternoon and her clothes are soaked through.

She needs to collect the carcass. She needs to skin the deer. On the hunting shows, they called it dressing the kill. As if this act of bones and hides and tendons is like dressing up for a party. Her father would have known how to halve and quarter an animal.

It is larger than she imagined. The shot had pierced an artery, making it messy. She remembers now how they said blood contaminates. She must skin it and drain it or the meat will spoil. She recites names. Shank. Rump. Backstrap. Words that used to drift like incantations from the campground televisions of her first years here. She racks her head, trying hard to think of other words.

NAMING
Ba, the physicist, who knew everything
about anatomy and galaxies and plants,
didn't know the names they called him.

Gutting

Like dog. Pig.
They were all called beasts.
I wasn't called Kim
when I reported Ba,
who hadn't actually burned a portrait
just forced it to the back of his cupboard.
How I jabbed the air with a book.
scarf around my throat like an idiot.
Ba's head shaved in hideous clumps.
They did the same for others
who wore lipstick, or played with birds,
read poetry or styled their hair loose.

Ba sent west on packed trains,
somewhere in the loess plains of Gansu.
I waited for the trains to bring him back.
There were no homecoming trains.
I grew to 175 cm. I graduated nursing school.
There were no homecoming trains.
I left for Hong Kong.
There were no homecoming trains.

Kim stands, unmoving for a long time. Unwilling to break the skin of inertia. Finally, she heaves the animal so the legs point up. She has no rope to hoist it above ground. She slits just above the anus, careful not to rupture the guts. It could poison her if the contents spilled over the meat. Her hands shake. The organs are still warm.

The skinning must be fast. The longer the body is insulated, the quicker bacteria develops. She must cool the body right away. But her hands slip. The pelt is musky. It does not skin easily like a rabbit. It is nothing like a rabbit.

Her father would know what to do with deer entrails. Oblong shapes, coils, lozenges. Slabs of purple, like afterbirth. Gelatinous, glutinous tendons. Shank. Rump. Backstrap. James would know what to do. Hands that could slice whale blubber splitting skin down to bone.

James—like her father—were people who knew the truth of things with certainty. His words run through her head, "The social organisation of whales is strong. When something terrible happens, the rest of the group won't leave. They don't abandon family." Kim, on the other hand, knows that she knows nothing.

Kim looks down at the mess of splayed out limbs and the belly full of still-warm organs. She talks herself through the topography of muscle. Shank. Rump. Backstrap. The muzzle wet, bloody. Using the names, she guides her knife. She dips her hands in wrist deep. The tideline of blood washes up her forearms, reaches past her elbows. She pulls everything out, scattering the warm mess around the deer carcass. She hopes the smell will lure Rutherford back to her through the maze of foliage, like organ talismans.

All that is left is the hollow cavity of the ribcage, like a shell curving inwards. She sits down, then eases backwards, wrapping herself inside. The bones seem to reach around shoulders, now bare. She covers the skins over her in a spongy warmth. All alone, she has succeeded in dressing the deer. The deer are invaders. Just like herself, they do not belong here. In the undergrowth far from the sea, Kim waits.

'Gutting' was first published in the online journal, **Hainamana** (2020).

Ting. J. Yiu (姚敏婷) was born in Hong Kong and immigrated to Auckland with her family when she was eleven. She holds BAs in both English Literature and Human Geography from the University of Otago, and an MA in Transnational Creative Writing from Stockholm University. She writes poetry, literary fiction and creative non-fiction. Her works have appeared in a variety of publications and online journals. Ting has been teaching creative writing since 2018, and, in 2019 founded The Writers' Collective where she leads writing workshops and holds seminars on creativity and craft. She is currently working on a short story collection and a polyphonic novel about the Chinese diaspora.

Acknowledgements

This book was put together first and foremost for teachers and students, to ripple out from schools into the world, and in this regard I would like to thank teachers Susana Carryer and Chris (Kit) Willett for their advice right at the beginning. This wouldn't be as well ordered or as interesting without them.

The unfortunate destination of so many kiwi short story collections and literary journals is the upper floors and the shut cupboards in libraries. But there they are well preserved and cared for by librarians, waiting for someone like me to request a towering stack of them. Thank you to all librarians in New Zealand for this service and especially the staff at Hamilton Central Library who brought out stack after stack of books to my small research table, helped me use the scanner, and let me take precious items to other floors (librarians have a strong rebellious streak. I recommend having one on your side when the zombies arrive!).

Thank you to established writer Alison Wong who couldn't herself be in the collection but championed and directed me to some wonderful emerging authors.

Also thank you to Christine Dale and Jenny Nagle at OneTree House. Publishing Aotearoa New Zealand books is done on a dollar in the rain, on a Sunday at midnight, in clothes that need mending while the cat needs feeding; in other words, it isn't easy; people aren't even that grateful, but it is a wonderful thing. This opportunity, and the many you have given me over my career, are precious things.

Finally thank you especially to our writers, all of them so generous with their time and talents. And thank you too to you, the reader. We are in a relationship, us writers and you – nau te rourou, naku te rourou, ka ora te manuhiri.

Elizabeth Kirkby-Mcleod